ALL RIG

ALSO BY MARGARET MALLORY

(Available in ebook, print, and audiobook)

THE DOUGLAS LEGACY
CAPTURED BY A LAIRD
CLAIMED BY A HIGHLANDER (coming soon)

THE RETURN OF THE HIGHLANDERS
THE GUARDIAN
THE SINNER
THE WARRIOR
THE CHIEFTAIN

ALL THE KING'S MEN
KNIGHT OF DESIRE
KNIGHT OF PLEASURE
KNIGHT OF PASSION

THE
GIFT
A Highland Novella

MARGARET
MALLORY

CHAPTER 1

Late 1441

They were burning witches.

Lily knew better than to dabble in the black arts, but with witch fever spreading through London like the plague, any woman who sold cures for headaches, warts, or love was at risk.

"Ouch!" Lily pricked her finger in her haste to stitch her gold coins into the boy's tunic she had acquired for her escape.

As she jerked on the tunic and breeches, she cursed the Duchess of Gloucester, who had attempted to murder the king with sorcery in hope of seeing the crown on her husband's fat head.

Not that Lily gave a farthing who was king, but why hadn't the woman simply poisoned him?

Thanks to the duchess's dance with the devil, gangs were roaming the streets hunting for witches. Many were shocked to learn that the duchess's co-conspirators in her witches' coven were priests and monks, but Lily had grown up as the child of a criminal. Evil did not surprise her.

She tilted her head to listen to the sounds in the dark street outside her shop. *Were they growing louder?* Following her instincts had saved her many times, and they were screaming for her to escape London until this witch-hunting frenzy passed.

Lily's heart raced as she stuffed her wild, curling red hair into the boy's cap. She quickly donned the rest of her disguise, stepping into the too-large boots and tossing the rough brown cloak over her shoulders.

1

An hour ago, she had picked the lock on the baker's door, crept past the sleeping family, and helped herself to the clothes that were hanging on a hook by the son's bed. She smelled faintly of yeast, but she was grateful it was not the fishmonger or the skinner who owed her for curing his boils.

That would teach the baker to pay his debts.

Hastily, she gathered small vials of the powders and potions that would be most difficult to replace and wrapped them in her extra pair of wool stockings. These she packed, along with a wineskin, a sharp blade, and a loaf of the baker's fine bread, into a worn leather bag, which she then slung over her shoulder.

At the door, she paused to take a last look at the shop where she had lived and worked since she was a child of seven. Her heart felt heavy as her gaze traveled over the neat rows of jars lining the shelves, the scrubbed pots hanging by the fire, and the fragrant bunches of drying herbs hanging from the rafters.

She did not fool herself that any of it would be here when she returned. She would have to start from scratch. In the two years since the old herbalist had died and passed the business on to her, Lily had developed a thriving trade. The old woman had taught her well, and Lily had a knack for reading people and uncovering their secrets—valuable skills in a healer.

Her success had led to several marriage proposals from neighboring merchants. She snorted. Romantics all of them. If the church charged her with consorting with demons—which generally involved committing acts too disgusting for anyone but the priests to imagine—not one of the merchants who had professed undying love would defend her.

The men of her family were worse. Even if they offered to help her, which was unlikely, they were unreliable liars and cheats. There was not one person in the entire city of London she was willing to entrust with her safety.

She locked her door, a futile gesture, and hid the key inside her sock as a promise to herself that she would return to her beloved shop. Christmas was not far off. Surely a month of advent festivities would divert the mobs' attention and make it safe to return.

Lily slipped silently through back alleys she'd known since childhood to make her way down to the River Thames. Her friends Linnet and Jamie had gone to live in the far north of England—

Northumberland, it was called. The wealthy couple had befriended her when she was a tiny girl, and they still came by the shop with their increasing brood on their rare trips to London. They had invited her many times to visit them.

Of course, neither she nor they believed she ever would.

When she reached the shore of the Thames, the heavy night fog that lay over the river engulfed her like a cold, damp shroud. Her steps sounded unnaturally loud in the still, thick air as she walked along the docks, and the dank smell of the river filled her nose. All she could see of the ships that lined the riverbank was the soft glow of their lanterns bobbing in the eerie mist.

She walked toward them, intent on taking the first ship sailing north.

***

"I'd rather travel to hell than to the Lowlands," Roderick muttered under his breath as he sharpened his dirks in preparation for the long journey. "Out of the thousands of warriors at his command, why did the Lord of the Isles choose me for this miserable task?"

Most likely, he was singled out because he could speak the language of the Lowlanders, which he learned while a prisoner there—an experience he did not wish to repeat. But a warrior did not say nay to his chieftain, particularly when his chieftain was the Lord of the Isles, who ruled over more of the Highlands than the Scottish king.

"That 'tis no' the reason he chose ye to carry his message to the Douglas chieftain," his grandmother said as she stirred a pot of fish stew over the hearth fire.

Roderick was long accustomed to his grandmother reading his thoughts, for she had the gift of *The Sight*. Growing up in a tiny cottage with the clan's seer had been awkward at times for a lad. Once he became a man, she generally respected his private thoughts. Still, he made an effort to keep his mind off the lasses when he visited her.

"Then why, pray tell, was I selected for this *special* honor, Seanmhair?" Roderick asked.

"You're one of his verra best warriors, and our chieftain has great trust in ye."

Roderick gave his grandmother a sideways glance. Though he knew she was proud of him, it was not in her nature to hand out compliments.

"And," she added after a long pause, "I advised him to send ye."

Roderick swallowed an oath. "Why would ye do that, Seanmhair?"

"A great clan like ours must have a powerful seer, and no one has been born to replace me," she said. "A few MacDonald lasses do have *The Sight*, but 'tis weak in 'em."

God only knew what that had to do with his grandmother recommending him for this miserable errand. He hoped her mind was not growing feeble, but she was as old as the mist.

"I'll be passing through the lands belonging to other clans on my journey," he said, as he strapped on his claymore sword and hoisted his leather bag over his shoulder. "Am I to look for a seer and steal her?"

He meant the question as a jest. He should have known better.

"I fear stealing this particular lass would be a mistake," his grandmother said with that strange, faraway look in her eyes. "Ye will have better luck if ye can persuade her to come, but bring her ye must."

He sighed and kissed her goodbye on the cheek. "God be with ye, Seanmhair. Remember, the chieftain himself is sending a boat to take ye to the Isle of Islay in a few days. I'll return in time to join ye there for the Yule celebrations."

His boat was waiting in the cove at the bottom of the cliff below her cottage. He'd already started down the steep steps that were cut into the side of the cliff when he heard her call to him over the wind. Looking up, he saw his grandmother leaning over the sheer rock face clutching a plaid about her shoulders.

"Mind ye don't fall!" he shouted.

She just leaned farther over the edge. Praise God, he had persuaded the stubborn woman to leave her lonely cliff-side cottage for the winter. On the chieftain's home isle of Islay, she'd always be well looked after when he was away.

"Ye won't find the lass ye need," she called down, "until ye stop looking for her."

Roderick loved her dearly, but he had no notion if his grandmother was still talking about a seer or wasting her breath harping on him again about taking a wife to replace the one who left him. He waved to let her know he'd heard what she said, for what that was worth, and prayed she would still be among the living when he returned.

***

The unrelenting wind made Lily's eyes water as she stared at the endless hills surrounding her. She had lived in London all her life and had no notion that the countryside went on forever like this. After walking for three days, it all looked the same.

Damn. She should have found how far north that ship was sailing before she sneaked on board. What sin had she committed that led God to punish her by sending her to Scotland?

Blindfold her and toss her out of a cart on any street corner in London, and she would know where she was and how to get her next meal. From the time she was a small child, she had traversed the dangerous streets of London unscathed. She could outwit degenerates of all types, from cutpurses to rapists.

Yet it appeared she would die of simple hunger and cold, defeated by these empty hills.

She had no idea if she was still walking in the direction of the border or going in circles. Continuing seemed pointless, and yet she forced herself to trudge on. She had ceased to feel her frozen hands and feet long ago, and her thoughts had grown sluggish. As a healer, she was aware that these were dangerous signs, but knowing did not help her one whit.

Her foot caught in a hole, sending her sprawling to the ground. Despite how weak she was from lack of food, she dragged herself back up. She swayed on her feet, mesmerized by how the wind moving through the grass looked like sea swells. She had not expected to enjoy sailing on the sea.

What happened after they tossed her off the ship? Though she tried, she could not remember.

She managed a few more steps before stumbling again. This time, she pitched forward and fell hard. She rolled downhill, her head bouncing on the ground again and again. When her body finally came to a halt, she lay facedown, stunned and dizzy.

Get up! Ye must keep moving!

5

Lily knew she should listen to the nagging voice in the back of her head. But she was so very tired… She had to rest…for just a little while…

CHAPTER 2

Roderick swept his gaze over the hills again. Watching for signs of an ambush was an ingrained habit that had saved his life more than once. He had delivered the message entrusted to him with no mishap. And now, praise God and all the angels in heaven, he was headed home to the Highlands.

Unfortunately, he was not traveling alone.

The Douglas chieftain, the 3rd Earl of Angus, must consider his reply to the Lord of the Isles dangerous, indeed, for he had insisted that half a dozen of his warriors accompany Roderick across the breadth of Scotland from his fortress, Tantallon Castle, to the western coast. If the secret missives between these two powerful men threatened the Crown, the Douglas chieftain had far more to fear if his fell into the wrong hands. The Lord of the Isles had the protection of mountains, sea, and thousands of warriors who felt no allegiance to the Scottish Crown.

Roderick spared a glance at the Douglas warriors. They may be allies for the time being, but that did not mean he had to like them. And he certainly knew better than to trust them.

These Lowlanders were too much like the English for Roderick's taste, and he detested the English. Their weapons shone bright, but these warriors were careless, talking and joking amongst themselves though they were no longer on Douglas lands. He reminded himself that he'd be rid of them in a couple of days—if he lived that long.

Roderick pulled his horse up and raised his hand to signal the Douglas men. He scanned the hills to the south, looking for what had pricked his attention.

"What is it?" Harold, the bulky leader of the Douglas men, asked and eyed him with suspicion.

"Someone is hiding in the tall grass over there," Roderick said, nodding toward a dark patch amidst the green.

"'Tis nothing but a rock."

Harold apparently suffered from poor eyesight.

"I'll have a look all the same," Roderick said. "You lads can ride ahead."

Roderick cantered across the hillside without waiting for a response. As he rode closer, the figure in the grass remained unnaturally still. This was someone in trouble, not a lookout for bandits or other troublemakers.

He dropped off the side of his horse beside the prone body. *Damn*, 'twas just a lad, and he looked dead.

Roderick knelt beside him and felt for a pulse. Relief swept through him when he felt the faint beat. The lad's skin was cold to the touch, but he was still alive. Moving quickly, he began rubbing the lad's back and legs to get his blood moving.

Whisky, the best cure for most ailments, would warm the lad from the inside. Roderick flipped him over and pulled out his flask. Beneath the dirt and scratches, the lad's face was young and beardless.

"Don't die on me," Roderick ordered as he slid his arm beneath the lad's narrow shoulders and raised him up to drink.

The frail body shivered in his arms. The poor lad was near frozen to death.

"Come, laddie, take a sip," Roderick said as he tipped the flask.

The boy coughed as the whisky slid down his throat, but he swallowed a healthy gulp. A good sign. Roderick drew in a deep breath and relaxed a wee bit. But then the lad's cap fell off.

Piles of flaming red curls spilled over Roderick's arm and onto the ground like a tumultuous river of fire. Roderick blinked, unable to take in this revelation all at once.

Good God, the lad is a lass.

Beneath the dirt, he could make out a sprinkling of freckles across her pale cheeks and an upturned nose. Her features were delicate, save for her full-lipped mouth, which, like her wild locks, bespoke of a wanton sensuality—or at least would make a man hope for it. *Ach*, how could he have mistaken this bonny lass for a lad?

She opened her eyes, and his world tilted again.

The lass lay utterly still in his arms, staring up at him with eyes as green as the glen after the spring rains and fringed by red-gold lashes that reminded him of sun streaks across a shimmering dawn sky.

He ought to comfort her, to tell her not to be frightened, but when he opened his mouth, nothing came out. When he tore his gaze away from her eyes to try to regain his bearings, it dropped unerringly to her red, parted lips, which did not help at all.

"You'll be all right now," he said, once he finally found his voice.

She nodded, showing no sign she feared him. If she trusted that easily, no wonder the lass had gotten herself into such trouble.

"Your people must live nearby," he said. "I'll take ye to them."

"I have no people here," she whispered.

"God's blood, you're English!" He could hardly believe his ears. He had spoken to her in Scots, which was essentially the same language, though the accent was different. "How did an English lass come to be so far from the border? And all by yourself?"

When confusion clouded her eyes, he cursed himself for pressing her so soon.

"I'd best feed ye first, aye?" He helped her sit up, then gave her a piece of dried venison from the bag tied to his belt. "Ye must be hungry."

She ate it like a starving creature. While her attention was focused on the venison, he continued his examination of her. She was a wee thing, with lovely, delicate hands. He could not discern her shape in the oversized clothes, which must have been her intent, but it was not hard to imagine that the beauty of her face extended to the rest of her.

"How old are ye?" he asked.

"Two and twenty," she said.

That much was a relief. At least he wasn't having untoward thoughts about a lass who was too young. But what in hell was he going to do with her? He had an important mission to complete for his chieftain, and he must not tarry. Yet he could not leave her here to die.

When she finished eating the small strip of venison, she leaned against him, as if exhausted from the effort. His heart did an odd flip.

"A bit more whisky will help, lass." He lifted the flask to her lips and held her close to keep her warm.

Thump-thump, thump-thump. At the sound of hoofbeats, he slammed her to the ground.

"I travel with strangers," he said an inch from her face. "'Tis best they not discover that ye are a lass. Understand?"

"Aye," she said, and her breath tickled his lips.

For a dangerous moment, he stared into her remarkable green eyes and forgot where he was and how he came to be lying half on top of her. By the saints, how could any man be fooled by her disguise? He picked up her cap and began stuffing her hair into it. If the others caught a glimpse of her long, wild locks, the chance of deceiving them would go from poor to none.

"No one else has found me out," she said, as if she'd heard his thoughts.

With deft fingers, she tucked the curls he'd missed out of sight under the cap.

He sat up in time to see the Douglas men appear over the hill. "Here they come."

As she craned her neck to see over the tall grass, she leaned against him, startling him with her touch. He wondered again why she trusted him so easily. She shouldn't. When she turned to look at him, her expression was alert, but not frightened, despite the half-dozen warriors who were nearly upon them.

"We've no time to agree upon a story," Roderick said, speaking quickly. "I'll tell them something. Just don't contradict me."

"I won't." She gave him a solemn wink, then closed her eyes and went limp in his arms.

"Jesu," he said under his breath as he looked down at her, "who are you?"

***

Lily was not on regular speaking terms with God, but she sent up a prayer of thanks that it was the handsome man with the bluest eyes she'd ever seen who found her, and not one of these other men. As she listened to their voices above her, she knew in her bones that she would not have been safe with any of them.

Her rescuer had hair as black as the devil and a startling number of weapons strapped to his tall, muscular frame. She should have been frightened by him, but when she awoke to those dark blue

10

eyes staring intently into hers, she saw kindness in them and trusted him at once.

"Who's the lad, Highlander?" one of the other men asked.

"How am I to know? He's too weak to speak," her rescuer said. "We'll have to take him with us until we can find someone to care for him."

The voices of the others rose, insisting that he "keep to the task" and "leave the lad behind." The Highlander simply waited until they ran out of words.

"Do as ye please," he told them, "but I won't leave a half-grown lad to die."

He scooped Lily off the ground, and the next thing she knew she was sitting in front of him on his horse. Her bag, which was still tied to her by its strap, came with her and slapped against her hip. Though she had ridden in a cart before, she'd never sat on a horse's back. It all happened so quickly that she barely managed to stifle a scream. A trifle late, she remembered to loll her head forward—and prayed her cap stayed in place.

"I'll take the lead," the Highlander shouted to the others, then he whispered in her ear, "We'll get some distance from them so we may speak freely. Hold on."

The sensation of his breath on her cheek and the deep rumble of his voice through her back made her slow to take in his words. An instant later, the Highlander's arm tightened around her waist, and she was slammed backward against his chest as the horse bolted forward.

Suddenly she was flying over the ground, with the grass a blur beneath her and her rescuer's body enfolding hers as if they were one. Her heart pounded and she felt breathless.

Had her ordeal addled her mind? She was on a horse with a wild Highlander, going God-knew-where with men even *he* did not trust, and yet she found it...*thrilling*.

It was not as if she had never been close to a man before. She had touched plenty of men, intimately. She had looked down their throats, felt their bellies for tumors, and applied poultices to their weeping wounds. Once, she'd even treated an infected cock. Now that was disgusting.

Despite all her experience as a healer, she was quickly discovering that having a healthy and handsome man's body touching hers from her head to her heels was an altogether different sensation. Of course, many women had told her as much when they came to her begging for love potions. But as a healer, she knew every sort of trouble men caused women, and she'd never met a man she thought was worth the risk.

After the Highlander slowed the horse to a walk, he handed her his leather pouch, which she opened to find hard oat biscuits and dried venison.

"Ye must eat some more," he said, "but do it slowly."

That was good advice, but her stomach had shrunk so from her ordeal that she doubted she could eat much anyway.

Each step the horse took caused the Highlander's thighs to rub against hers, which in turn sent tingles of awareness coursing through her body. She liked the sensation far more than she wished. While she could never abide the thought of being chained to a husband for life, she began to understand why a woman would take a lover.

"Feeling better now, lass?" the Highlander asked, the rumble of his voice sending another unexpected thrill through her.

"I am, thank you."

She looked down to find the leather pouch in her lap was empty. She had been so distracted by the unusual course of her thoughts that she had eaten it all without realizing it.

"You're warm enough?"

She swallowed. "Thoroughly warm."

"Then perhaps ye can tell me now how an English lass came to be wandering alone in the hills of Scotland?"

She could not very well admit that she left London for fear of being burned as a witch.

"'Tis a long story," she said, making her voice faint, "and I fear I'm still a bit weak."

"Hmmph. Ye must at least tell me where ye were headed, or I cannot help ye get there."

Now that her blood was moving again and she had some nourishment, Lily remembered her journey only too well. When the boat left her in Edinburgh, she should have stayed there. She knew how to survive in a city, even an unfamiliar one where the people had such an odd way of speaking English.

"I was on my way to Northumberland," she said, deciding it was safe to tell him that much.

"Walking. All that way. By yourself." The Highlander added something in a language she could not understand, which she surmised was a curse.

"How else was I to get there?" She certainly was not getting on a ship again after what happened the first time. "I heard tell of a famous healer who lives near the border. As I'd be passing by, I intended to stop and pay her a visit."

"Why did ye wish to see this healer?" he asked. "Are ye in need of a cure?"

Tension vibrated from his body, a warning that her answer was important to him, though she could not imagine why.

"I hoped to learn new cures from her," she said, deciding to tell him the truth, for lack of a better idea. "You see, I'm a healer myself."

***

Women who had the gift of *The Sight* were very often healers.

His grandmother's last words returned to Roderick like a thump on the head. *Ye won't find the lass ye need until ye stop looking for her.*

He had stopped looking for her. Despite his suspicion that his grandmother was confused when she spoke about his journey in the same breath as the clan's need for a seer, he had been alert to the possibility of meeting a seer while he traveled through the Highlands on his way to the Douglas stronghold. As soon as he crossed into the Lowlands, however, he put the idea out of his head.

The Sight was a magical gift, so it never occurred to him that the gift would be strong in a Lowlander. An English seer seemed an utter impossibility. No one lacked imagination like the English.

Yet he could not dismiss the notion that this lass dressed in breeches could be the seer his grandmother foretold. Finding an English lass lying on a Scottish hillside so many miles from the border was strange enough to have a touch of magic about it. When the lass awoke in his arms, her vivid green eyes cast an enchantment upon him, for certain, though he suspected that was the common sort of women's magic that caused men trouble every day.

13

He considered asking her outright if she had *The Sight*, but he did not believe she'd be forthcoming about being a Seer. Even in her weakened state, she had been careful not to tell him why or how she came to be wandering alone through Scottish hills.

"What is your name, lass?" he asked, deciding to start with an easy question and work his way up to it. "I am Roderick, son of Teàrlach of the MacDonalds and Muireall of the Clanranalds." He left out prior generations, though being a good Highlander, he could recite them back a couple hundred years without straining his memory.

He leaned to the side to get a better look at her as he waited for her to respond in kind. She had a soothing stillness about her that he admired, but he wanted answers now.

"Lily," she said.

A lass who would not even share her family name had secrets she intended to hold on to.

"'Tis a lovely name," he said. "Where is your home, Lily?"

She paused so long this time that he had given up expecting a response when she said, "London."

"*London?* Ach, that's a fair distance." He had assumed she lived near the border. Now it was an even greater mystery how she had come to be on that hillside. "I fear it won't be easy to get ye home, lass, especially with the winter storms upon us."

"I can wait."

She must be running away from something. Or someone. She had put a good deal of distance between herself and London, and she was not anxious to return home.

"What am I to do with ye in the meantime?" he asked, though he was already forming a plan.

"Set me on a road to Northumberland," she said. "I have a friend there."

"Are ye dimwitted? I'm no' leaving ye along a damned road to die of the cold, if you're not murdered first." He took a deep breath. "Northumberland is a long way from here, and I'm traveling in the other direction."

"Then leave me in the first town we come to," she said. "I'll do fine anywhere there are folk who need healing and are willing to trade for it."

"Hmmph." As if he could leave her to fend for herself among strangers—and Lowlanders at that.

"I'll have ye know that I'm a much sought after healer in London," she said.

Then why did she leave? And why, after nearly meeting her death here, was she not begging to go home? Once again he wondered what awaited her in London that she preferred to risk her fate with strangers.

He took this as another sign that she was, indeed, the lass he was supposed to bring home to serve his clan. Whether she was or not, he was responsible for her now.

CHAPTER 3

"Time to wake up, lass."

The low whisper in her ear woke Lily with a start. It took her a long moment to recall how she came to be leaning against a man's chest and why the seat beneath her was rocking. She could not say which surprised her more—that she fell sound asleep on a horse's back or that she did it enfolded in this huge Highland warrior's arms.

She must have slept a long time. The hills were silhouetted against the sunset, and the sky was rapidly growing dark. She shuddered as she remembered the previous night, when she had curled up, hungry and freezing, on a barren hillside.

"Ye can go back to sleep after we set up camp and have our supper," he said, squeezing her arm. "Until then, ye must have your wits about ye."

"I will."

She sat up straight and felt around the edges of her hat to be sure no long strands had escaped, then leaned to the side to look behind them. The dark line of Douglas warriors following them through the valley looked menacing in the fading light.

"I don't trust these men," she told him.

"But ye trust me," he said. "Why?"

She shrugged. "I just do."

He was quiet for a long while, as if contemplating her reply. Let him wonder. She was not telling a man who prided himself on being a fierce warrior that she trusted him because he had kindness in his eyes.

"If these men discover you're English, it will make them uneasy," he said. "Uneasy men are dangerous."

"Then I'll speak the way they do," she said, doing her best to mimic their accent.

"Better not attempt it," the Highlander said with a laugh.

The low rumble of his chest vibrating against her back was oddly comforting, though she failed to see the humor in her situation.

16

"I'll tell them you're a Highlander," he said, "and that ye only have the Gaelic."

"The what?"

"The language of the Highlands," he said. "When I speak to ye, just nod and pretend ye understand."

"I don't mean to insult you," she said, "but that sounds like a poor plan to me."

She regretted speaking so bluntly. But instead of being angry at the insult, he laughed again, a loud, reassuring sound that spilled over her and left inexplicable sparks of joy in its wake.

***

Roderick was grateful that nightfall came early this close to Yuletide and laid out his extra plaid for Lily well outside the circle of firelight. Pretending she was too weak to fetch her own meal, which was not far from the truth, he brought her supper to her there. The Douglas men would soon forget about "the lad" asleep in the dark behind them and quit grumbling about Roderick bringing "him" along.

He wanted to avoid trouble with them if he could, especially now that he had the lass to worry about. To make the men feel more at ease with him, he exchanged tales, threw dice, and drank with them through the long evening until finally all the Douglas men lay down for the night, rolled up in their cloaks and blankets.

Roderick stretched out on the ground next to Lily, careful not to wake her. Away from the fire, there was a sharp bite in the night air. They would wake up to frost in the morning. He lay awake long into the night, alert to every sound—the snorts of the Douglas men, the wind in the branches overhead, the hoot of an owl, and the soft breathing of the lass who slept an arm's reach away.

Who was she? Did she have a man she was running from? Was she the seer his clan needed? What did she look like under her ill-fitting clothes? Though the last question was the least important, it occupied most of his thoughts.

He must have finally dozed off, for he awoke with a start when Lily rolled into him. It was lucky he realized that the soft body pressed into his was Lily's, or his blade might be between her ribs. The thought made him break out into a sweat.

17

The lass must be cold. Still, he could not risk letting her stay tucked against him, lest one of the others discover them like this. With a sigh of regret, he eased her a safe distance away.

The day had been long, and this time he fell into a deep sleep. He awakened slowly, dragged from a dream of a green-eyed lass who smiled up at him as she lay in his arms. Sensing she was about to tell him something important, he fought to hold on to the dream long enough to hear it...

Roderick's eyes flew open. *By the saints*, she had done it again. The full length of her body was pressed against his—and now, the sky was turning gray with the coming dawn. He covered Lily's mouth and leaned over her.

"Ye cannot lie next to me as if we're lovers, or they'll know you're a lass," he said in a hushed voice.

The thought of them being lovers sent a surge of lust through his veins and made him suddenly aware of every inch that their bodies touched. He would swear he could feel her heart beat against his.

When she nodded beneath his hand, he paused a moment too long before releasing her. Then he sat up and glanced around the camp. The others were still asleep, *praise God*. He drew in a deep breath.

"Quickly now," he whispered, "go take care of your needs before the others are up and about."

He pointed to the thick shrubs that grew along the burn and watched her disappear into them. If it would not cause the Douglases to suspect some sort of treachery on the part of his chieftain, Roderick would steal away with her while they still slept.

The other men soon began to stir, so he got up and rekindled the fire. What was taking the lass so damned long? After nearly dying yesterday, surely she would know better than to run off on her own. But could she have gotten lost? The burn was only a few yards away, but the lass obviously had an abysmal sense of direction.

The Douglases were all up and ready for breakfast when he finally saw Lily's small figure appear through the bushes. The tension between his shoulders eased until he noticed the distinctly feminine way she walked, swaying her hips and minding where she put her feet to avoid the mud, rather than charging ahead like a lad.

When she joined him by the fire, she looked up and gave him a bright smile.

Ach, she had scrubbed her face clean. No lad of thirteen would do that. Worse still, her face looked even lovelier without the dirt to hide it.

***

"For the love of God," the Highlander hissed at her, "why did ye wash your face?"

What had she done wrong? To cover her confusion—and an unexpected stab of hurt—Lily spun away from him and sat on the plaid blanket that had served as her bed. Roderick could not truly be angry with her for washing, could he? No, that was ridiculous. He must still be upset about waking with his arms wrapped around her. Obviously, he blamed her, as men always blame women, though it was his fault entirely.

She would have pointed this out to him, if she were allowed to speak around the others.

As she watched the men line up for scoops of porridge from the pot on the fire, she wondered who Roderick had been dreaming about when he pulled her against him. Evidently he was accustomed to sleeping with someone. Poisonous tendrils of envy squeezed her heart.

She would never admit it to a living soul, but she had awakened long before he did this morning and lay still, barely breathing, so as not to wake him and end the embrace. Given the Highlander's size and overbearing nature, she should have felt suffocated, trapped. Instead, she had felt truly safe for the first time in weeks.

What must it be like to wake in this warrior's arms every day? To feel protected. Wanted. Even cherished.

Someone nudged her, startling her from her reverie. When she turned to find Roderick seated beside her and peering at her as if he could read her thoughts, her cheeks flamed hot. Her embarrassment gave way to hunger, however, as soon as she noticed he was holding out a steaming bowl of the porridge.

Her body had not yet recovered from going without food for so long, and the smell made her ravenous. Only after she had scraped the last spoonful from the bowl did she notice that Roderick was not eating. Traveling alone, he would carry only one bowl, and he had given it to her first. The kindness of the gesture made her immediately forgive him for snarling at her about washing her face, and she offered him a smile as she handed him his empty bowl and spoon.

Now why in heaven's name was the man glaring at her again? She felt around the edge of her cap to make sure no long strands had escaped. Nothing was amiss. She glanced around the circle of men around the fire to find that a big brute with mean eyes was staring at her. From what she had overheard of the men's conversation, his name was Harold, and he was the leader of the Douglas group.

"As soon as ye can slip away without being noticed," Roderick said in a low voice without looking at her, "I want ye to hide until this is over."

Until what is over?

"The lad has a pretty face," Harold said. "A man with imagination could pretend he was a lass."

"Let him be." Roderick spoke in a lazy tone and leaned back on one elbow. "If you've that much imagination, go bother the sheep."

Harold tossed his cup onto the ground and sprang to his feet.

Panic jangled through Lily's limbs. The hulking Douglas warrior had murder in his eyes. She hoped Roderick would quickly apologize for insulting the man. Instead, he looked bored.

"By now," Roderick said, "I suppose the poor sheep hide when they see your ugly face coming."

"I don't fook sheep!" Harold shouted, clenching his fists.

"Call it lovemaking, do ye?" Roderick said, and laughed.

Harold's face turned a deeper shade of scarlet, and he charged Roderick like a bull. Before he planted his first step, the Highlander was on his feet wielding his huge two-handed sword. He blocked Harold's first jarring blow with time to spare. Lily blinked, not quite believing anyone could move that quickly.

The other men gathered around, shouting encouragement to Harold. "Stick your blade in him!" "Knock him on his arse!"

Lily remembered Roderick's warning to hide and scurried into the bushes. Her heart was in her throat as she watched the two men go back and forth across the grass, swords clanking. She had witnessed plenty of fistfights and stabbings, but she had never watched two skilled warriors do battle. It was utterly terrifying.

Harold was a giant of a man, with a barrel chest and grotesquely thick arms and legs. Fueled by rage, he swung his sword with a blunt force meant to pound his opponent into submission.

Please, God, don't let him kill my Highlander.

Guilt drenched her. She had caused this fight, though unknowingly. Her courage wavered, and she squeezed her eyes shut. But she could not escape the sounds of the fight. The shouts and grunts were loud in her ears, and the relentless *clang, clang, clang* of the swords reverberated up her spine. Unable to bear not knowing how her defender fared, she opened her eyes—and from that moment, she could not take them off Roderick.

She should have known her Highlander would fight like this. He was male beauty in motion. Lean and muscular, he moved with a stunning grace that made his opponent appear lumbering and ungainly. And while Harold fought with a crazed fury, her Highlander fought with a cold, deadly calm. She watched the muscles of his shoulders and back bunch and release with each smooth, sure stroke.

The shouts of the other Douglases waned as it became clear that the fight was going against their man. Harold was breathing like a dog that had been run too hard, while Roderick looked as if he could swing his sword all day long.

Roderick shot a glance in her direction, as if to reassure himself of her safety. Lily gasped as one of the Douglases took advantage of his momentary lapse to thrust a sword low in his path. Making it look effortless, Roderick leaped over the blade, and while his feet were off the ground, he hit the offender with the flat of his sword. Lily turned her head to watch the man fly backward.

By the time she whipped her gaze back to the fight, Harold was flat on his back and looking up the length of Roderick's sword. *How did he do that?* Keeping the point of his sword at Harold's throat, Roderick stared down the Douglas men who were circled about him until each one took a step back.

Lily had known instinctively from the first moment she looked into his eyes that he would not harm her. But now, as he stood fearless and threatening, though greatly outnumbered, she believed this fierce Highlander could protect her from any danger she was likely to face in this harsh, unfamiliar land.

What she did not yet understand was *why* he was willing to protect her.

***

Now that he had defeated their strongest warrior, Roderick doubted any of the other Douglases would challenge him. Still, there were six of them, and they were riled up. It would cause him a lot less trouble in the end if he did not have to kill them.

"Have ye forgotten I carry a message from your chieftain?" Roderick asked the men who were surrounding him. "He'll no' be pleased if it's not safely delivered."

From the corner of his eye, he caught another glimpse of Lily in the bushes and was relieved she was out of the way, in case his attempt to calm the Douglas men failed. Settling disputes with words was not one of his strengths.

"We could deliver the message ourselves," one of the men said, but he took a step back when Roderick smiled at him.

"The Lord of the Isles is my cousin, and ye know how we Highlanders feel about blood ties." It was true they were cousins, though three or four times removed. "But if ye wish to be buried in the Highlands, there's no lovelier place on God's green earth."

"He wouldn't touch us," another man said, sticking his jaw out. "We've all heard that your Highland custom of hospitality toward guests is unbreakable."

"Ach, my cousin would never murder ye inside his home. That would be wrong," Roderick said, shaking his head. "However, any manner of accident might befall ye on your long journey home."

Tension rippled through the men until Harold, who was still on his back, emitted a loud guffaw.

"So much for the famed Highland courtesy," Harold choked out between laughs. "Now get the hell off me!"

Roderick took his foot off Harold's chest and helped him up. Soon, they were all joking and passing a jug of whisky.

"That was a good fight, aye?" Harold said, slapping him on the back. "But next time, ye won't be so lucky."

Next time, I'll cut your throat. Roderick clinked his cup against Harold's and tossed back another dram of whisky.

Though he was not fond of drinking before his morning porridge was settled, he hoped it would help with his plan to rid himself of the Douglases.

"As ye can see, your chieftain's message is safe with me," he said. "I know ye take your duty to heart, but why waste your time escorting me when ye could be enjoying yourself?"

"I've no doubt ye can protect the message on your own," Harold said after wiping his mouth on his filthy sleeve. "But we've nothing better to do, and we can't return too soon."

"Fine with me." Roderick shrugged and paused before speaking again. "But we'll be out of whisky soon, and there's a lively tavern in the village of Cumnag, a mile south of here."

Roderick took his turn taking a pull on the jug while he waited for Harold to take the bait.

"Does this tavern have a woman a man can buy with a coin?" Harold asked, his grin displaying several rotted teeth.

"Aye, a pretty plump one," Roderick said with a wink.

***

How much could these Scots drink? Lily was stiff with cold from crouching in the bushes as she watched them through the branches. One moment they were set on murdering each other, and the next they were drinking like old friends. And it was barely past dawn.

If she wanted to spend the day hiding from drunken men, she could have stayed in London and visited her family.

The bushes offered scant protection from the damp wind whipping through the valley. Her eyelids were practically frozen open by the time the men finally began packing up to leave. After another round of backslapping and boasts, the Douglases mounted their horses and rode off, weaving in their saddles.

Lily emerged from her hiding place and went to stand beside Roderick, who was still packing up his horse.

"We're rid of the Douglases." He spoke without turning.

"Good," she said, though she was not entirely sure if he had spoken to her or the horse. "Are you too drunk to ride?"

Roderick spared her a scornful sideways glance, then returned his attention to the horse.

"Well, are you?" she asked. "If so, you must instruct me on how to guide the animal."

23

The horse pawed the ground and rolled his eyes at her in a remarkable imitation of his master.

"Alas, I am stone sober," Roderick muttered under his breath. "And what kind of man cannot ride drunk?"

Apparently, he was the sort who could. She had begun to believe this Highlander could do whatever he put his mind to. Reassured, she went to fetch the blanket she'd slept on and rolled it up.

"I'm sorry if I was the cause of that fight," she said.

"'Twas bound to happen." Roderick took the blanket from her and tied it to the saddle. "Harold had been spoiling for a fight since the start of the journey. I was happy to give it to him."

"Ye weren't afraid?"

That earned her another scornful glance.

"Not even a little?" she asked. "That brute Harold's neck is thicker than my waist."

"I imagine it is." Roderick gave her his full attention this time, giving her body a slow perusal that drove the chill from her bones like a roaring fire.

When he lifted his gaze to hers, his eyes were a dark midnight blue that bespoke of sin and mystery. They drew her in until she found herself tilting toward him like a weak fence.

He is going to kiss me. Of their own accord, her eyelids fluttered closed. Her heart thudded in her chest as she waited for his lips to touch hers.

"Harold is strong, but he lacks stamina and discipline."

Lily snapped her eyes open and was mortified to find that Roderick was leaning under the horse's belly, adjusting the saddle.

"While I've been training with a claymore since I could lift one," he continued, and gave the saddle a tug, "and fighting in battles since I was thirteen."

Had she imagined that Roderick wanted to kiss her? She looked down at herself in the dirty boy's clothing. Aye, she must have, for it would take a violator of sheep like Harold to find her appealing like this. Still, it was strange. Her instincts about people were usually so good.

She told herself it was fortunate Roderick had no thought of kissing her. She faced enough trouble without that. And yet, a sour disappointment curdled in her stomach.

When he straightened and brushed his hands, a shock of black hair fell over one eye. A high-pitched sound nearly escaped her throat. By the heavens, he was a dangerously handsome man.

"So, Highlander," she said, forcing her attention back to the conversation with some difficulty, "you were certain from the start of the fight that you would prevail?"

"Aye," he said. "The challenge was to make the fight last long enough so as not to humiliate him."

"You care about Harold's feelings?" She blinked at him. This was hard to credit.

"Ach, no." He gave a short laugh. "But insulting the Douglases would not serve my chieftain and clan."

Lily would do well to remember that duty, and not emotion, ruled the Highlander's heart. He had not permitted anger to impair his judgment in a fight, and he would not lose his wits over a woman.

But she feared she might be losing hers. When he put his hands on her waist to lift her onto the horse, that dizzying sensation took hold of her again. Long after he set her on the beast, she felt the imprint of his hands burned onto her skin.

Weakness for a man was the most common ailment that led women to seek her cures. Lily had believed herself immune. She was stunned to find that she was falling prey to the malady, especially for a wild Highlander she'd known less than a day.

The conclusion was inescapable. He had bewitched her.

She did not know how he'd done it—and she doubted he even meant to—but there was only one sure cure. As soon as she could safely do so, she must part from her blue-eyed Highlander with no hope of ever seeing him again.

Sadness descended upon her like a weight. Good heavens, she had the illness worse than she thought.

CHAPTER 4

Usually a good fight, like a good swiving, left Roderick relaxed, but he felt on edge. The lad's clothes Lily wore did nothing to disguise the tantalizing feel of her shapely arse between his thighs. When he was not imagining her naked, he was wondering what she was thinking. She had not said a word for miles. He'd never known a lass who could keep silent for so long. It was unnatural.

"You can leave me at the first town we reach," she said.

Learning that she'd spent the morning planning her departure worsened his already foul mood.

"How much longer before we come to one?" she said, sounding damned anxious.

"If all goes well, we'll reach Ayr tomorrow."

"*Tomorrow?* Are there no towns before this Ayr?" she asked. "I don't wish to be a burden on you any longer than I must."

"You're not a burden, damn it," he said, "and there are no other towns."

He was not about to abandon her in Ayr. Whether his grandmother was right or no about this lass, Lily would be better off wintering in the isles with the MacDonalds, where he could ensure her safety.

"Your husband must be worried about ye," he said. "Have ye left him for good, or do ye plan to return to him once ye feel you've tortured him enough?"

The question of whether she was married had been burning in his mind. He told himself he had a duty to find out. If Lily was the seer he was supposed to bring home to serve his clan, he must know what obstacles lay in his path.

"I have no husband," she said.

Was she lying? "At two and twenty, ye ought to have one."

"Ought I, now?" she said with a laugh in her voice.

"Aye." He stifled a groan when the motion of the horse caused her backside to rock against his crotch.

"I can put food on my table myself," she said. "What would I want with a husband?"

"To keep ye warm at night." As soon as he said it, the vivid memory of waking with her pressed against him came into his head. He imagined what that might have led to if they had not been surrounded by damned Douglases…

"I don't need to be wed to have a man for *that*," she said.

Roderick did not like her answer—no matter that he had been picturing her naked beneath him without the benefit of pledges.

"Ye need a man to protect ye," he said, though he did not know why he was arguing with her. "A husband will put your life before his."

"Ha, not the men I know," she said. "Besides, I can take care of myself."

"I saw how ye take care of yourself," he said. "I suppose ye were just taking a wee nap on the hillside when I found ye?"

When she shivered against his chest, he regretted reminding her of the state in which he had found her. He suppressed a ridiculous urge to wrap his arms tightly around her and kiss her neck.

"What was your plan once ye found that healer on the border?" he asked, though they both knew she would never have made it that far.

"I imagined her as a kindly old woman who would teach me her ways of healing and invite me to stay for as long as I liked." She gave a light laugh. "I must have gone a bit mad from hunger, for I had a clear picture in my head of the two of us decorating her cottage with greenery and cooking a delicious Christmas feast."

Judging from the longing in Lily's voice when she spoke of this healer she'd never met, he suspected there was an old woman back in London that she missed. That gave him an idea for how he could persuade her to travel with him to his clan.

"Whoever this Lowlander healer is," he said, "I can promise ye she doesn't possess half the gift my grandmother has."

Lily spun around to look at him. "Your grandmother is a healer?"

"Aye." Roderick had a difficult time concentrating with those green eyes staring at him in such close proximity. "She is famous throughout the Highlands for her gift."

His grandmother was a healer, but what she was famed for was *The Sight*. It would be for her to determine if Lily was the one fated to take her place—and if Lily was, to persuade her to stay.

Once Roderick delivered this Sassenach healer to his clan, his duty would be done.

***

"Show me where it pains you," Lily said.

After Roderick translated the phrase into Gaelic, she repeated it back to him. He had shown remarkable patience in teaching her simple phrases she would need to ply her trade.

"Ye have a good ear for our language," he said.

If she learned quickly, it was because the words sounded so appealing when they rolled off Roderick's tongue. Still, she could not learn much in a day. Fortunately, a healer relied on her observations as much as what she was told. She would get by.

All the same, she was glad Roderick seemed to have slowed their pace. She was not anxious to arrive in Ayr. She was not as confident as she pretended at the prospect of spending the winter in an unfamiliar place where she knew no one, but that was not the sole cause of this unease gnawing in the pit of her stomach. Though she tried to persuade herself otherwise, she dreaded having to part from her Highlander.

She felt safe with Roderick, and no one had made her feel safe in a long time.

The beauty of the Scottish landscape had been lost on her when she was wandering alone, lost and hungry. But now, as she looked at the lush green hills surrounding them, with their streams and endless tiny waterfalls, it seemed to her that each valley they rode through was more beautiful than the last.

"This rain won't last long," Roderick said when a cold drizzle began to fall. "But we can't have ye freezing to death, now can we?"

He wrapped his plaid around them both and pulled her close. With a small sigh, she leaned back and let herself enjoy this small respite before she was on her own again. She watched the countryside drift by, wrapped in his warmth, as they rode down the rain-sodden trail between ever-taller hills.

Roderick was the sort of man, rare in her world, who would make any woman feel safe. With his ruggedly handsome face and tall, lean, muscular body, he would have no shortage of women eager to share his bed.

But was there one he loved? Not that it mattered. She would never see him again after he left her in Ayr on the morrow.

"You asked if I have a husband," she said. "I suppose you have a wife and a babe or two waiting at home?"

"Nay."

For no good reason, Lily was pleased by his answer. But his sharp tone also piqued her curiosity.

"Did ye have a wife once?" she asked, taking a guess.

"'Tis too long a tale," he said in a tone meant to close the subject.

Of course, she was dying to hear it now. Listening to how he had broken some poor woman's heart would remind her that he was like other men. Most likely, he had thrown out his wife for some imagined infraction or because he tired of her.

"I prefer a long tale," she said, turning on the horse so she could see his face.

"Ye can't always have what ye want," he said. "And sit still. You're bothering the horse."

"I'll be satisfied with the short version," she said.

When he was quiet for a long time, she feared she had ruined the easy rapport that had grown between them. She was about to apologize when he finally spoke.

"I did have a wife," he said. "She left me."

What woman would leave him? The only reason Lily could conceive of was that he had been unfaithful. That was the usual cause.

"Why did she leave?" Lily knew she should leave it alone, but she could not seem to help herself.

"I was gone a long time," he said. "She tired of waiting for me."

"Where were you?" she asked, and wondered if he'd been off drinking and whoring.

"I was held captive in a Lowlander's dungeon."

"Your wife deserted you while you were imprisoned?" She was so outraged she could hardly get the words out.

29

"They had me chained to the wall in the hole, so it was some time before I was able to escape," he said, as though he blamed himself. "I was gone all winter."

"You're better off without her." Lily turned in the saddle again and rested her hand on his arm. "But, Roderick, are you not still bound to this woman?"

"Under Highland custom, either husband or wife may quit the marriage at the end of one year," he said. "I can have no complaint against the lass. And I don't."

He said the last words with force, but Lily did not believe him. His wife's departure had troubled him greatly. He must have loved her.

Did he love her still? The woman was worthless, but as a healer, Lily knew well that neither love nor desire was guided by reason.

CHAPTER 5

Roderick stopped for the night along the shore of the Firth of Clyde long before darkness fell. After snaring a rabbit for their dinner and gathering moss and wood for a fire, he stood at the water's edge listening to the lap of the waves. In the fading twilight, he could see the dark shapes of the cottages of Ayr dotting the coastline to the north. He could have easily reached the town tonight.

But he was not taking Lily to Ayr.

He had a boat hidden in the brush not far from where he stood and clansmen waiting for him across the Firth. The night was cold, but unusually clear for December. He could have sailed across tonight.

But he was not crossing the Firth tonight either.

He needed one night to persuade Lily to go with him to the Isle of Islay. Whether he persuaded her or not, she was getting in that boat with him in the morning.

And if he were honest, he *wanted* this one night alone with Lily. Not that he expected anything from her, though a man could always hope. He could not explain what drew him to her, or why he dreaded leaving her on Islay, where she would be safe and cared for.

He wanted one night with her when he did not have to be on his guard, waiting for the Douglases to discover she was English and a lass. One night when he could sit and talk with her by the fire without another soul in sight.

One night when he did not need to pretend he did not want her.

***

"Cold?" Roderick asked when Lily joined him.

Without waiting for her answer, he wrapped his plaid around her shoulders. They stood side by side in comfortable silence for a long while, staring out at the water.

"'Tis so different here," she murmured, struck by the beauty of the sea and the hills touched by the glow of the sunset. She bent down to dip her fingers in the clear water, which bore as much resemblance to the brown, smelly Thames as she did to this Highlander.

"It must seem quiet to ye, after your life in London," he said.

"Aye." She was so accustomed to the ceaseless noise, foul odors, and crowded streets of the city that she never noticed them. When she returned, she would miss the fresh smell of the wind in her face and this soothing silence, broken only by the occasional bird's cry or animal scurrying through the brush.

"Is it like this where you live?" she asked.

"The mountains are higher, the grass greener, and the sea wilder," he said.

Hard to imagine, but it must be still more beautiful there. She almost wished she could see it.

"There are more sheep than people," he said. "At this time of year, there are no crops to tend to and the winter storms keep the men at home with their families, unless there's fighting to be done."

For London shopkeepers, seasons made little difference in their work, and the fighting was drunken brawls in taverns.

"'Tis no surprise," he added with a chuckle in his voice, "that a great many babes are conceived this time of year."

His remark made her recall waking in his arms and sent her imagination down a dangerous road.

"Ach, you're shivering. I'll get a fire started to warm ye up." Roderick put an arm around her and led her to sit on a fallen log.

Lily buried her chin in his plaid and breathed in deeply as she watched him arrange the moss and wood he had gathered earlier. The plaid smelled of earth, wood smoke, and him.

"I'll clean and cook that hare ye caught," she said, and started to get up.

"No need." He cocked a smile at her. "Or don't ye like my cooking?"

"You're a fine cook," she said, feeling useless.

Despite everything being wet from the recent rains, he had the fire burning bright in no time. Then he skinned the hare, fashioned a spit for it from a stick, and set it to roasting over the fire, all with practiced ease and far faster than she could have. She admired such unusual self-sufficiency in a man.

And yet she began to wonder if his wife had left him because she felt unnecessary.

"You seem to be good at everything you set your hand to," she said.

"Oh, I do try, lass," he said, and flashed her a look that sizzled hotter than the flames of the fire.

He was clearly referring to more than his cooking skills, and her cheeks flushed. When he turned back toward the fire, her gaze lingered on the strong planes of his face in the warm glow of the firelight. He was the most beautiful man she'd ever seen.

Even while simply turning a spit over the fire, there was an untamed quality about him that sent her blood rushing through her veins. When Roderick looked up and caught her staring at him, their gazes locked and held across the fire. The flames licked at the corner of her vision and seemed to heat her from inside.

God help her, this Highlander was like a potent elixir of temptation.

***

After they finished eating, he and Lily sat a foot apart on the plaid staring into the fire, while the tension between them felt like a fraying rope that was pulled too tight. On Roderick's side, it was fraying to the breaking point. He had been tortured by her soft body rubbing against his for two long days on horseback. And last night, he had slept within arm's reach of her, yearning for her.

Unless he was badly mistaken, Lily shared his desire. She had spoken as if she'd had many lovers—*I don't need a husband for that*—so there was no reason for them not to indulge in a night of pleasure. Still, Roderick resisted the temptation to pull her into his arms. Lily was dependent on him for her safety, so he needed to be certain she wished to act on the hunger flaming between them.

He ignored the desire pounding through his veins as best he could and set his mind to the subtle battle of persuading her to come with him to Islay.

"'Tis nearly the longest night of the year." And he knew what he'd like to do with it. He took a deep breath and forced himself to focus on his plan. "It will be Yuletide soon."

Lily looked relieved that he had raised what appeared to be a benign topic. "How do you Highlanders celebrate it?" she asked.

"The women make special foods, and we hang greenery about our homes—including mistletoe for kissing." He gave her a

33

sideways glance that made her breath catch. "Everyone gathers together for days of feasting."

"That doesn't sound so different from how we English celebrate the Advent season," she said.

"I suspect ye might find some of our other customs barbaric," he said. "We're good Christians, but we remember the Old Ways."

"Barbaric?" she asked, her eyes sparkling. "Tell me."

"We build great bonfires," he said, spreading his arms wide, "dance, make music, drink, and listen to long tales."

"I can see you have fond memories of them," she said with a soft expression.

"Ye should come with me to the Isle of Islay for the Yuletide," he said. "The Lord of Isles, the great chieftain of the MacDonalds who rules over all the Western Isles and most of the rest of the Highlands, will be there. The celebrations will be grand, with mountains of food and the best musicians in all the Highlands."

Lily met his suggestion with silence and pressed her lips into a stubborn line, but he thought he saw longing in her eyes. He ignored a twinge of guilt over not telling her his true purpose. Whether Lily was destined to be his clan's next seer or no, she would be better off wintering with his clan, where he could ensure her safety.

"I know how ye like long tales," he said, giving her a wink. "There's sure to be plenty of those."

"In *Gaelic*," she said.

"All the better for learning it."

"What about those winter storms ye said would keep me here?" she asked, cocking her head.

"Sailing through the islands isn't nearly as dangerous as on the open sea," he explained. "There are plenty of places for a boat to shelter during a storm."

"Going there would take me even farther away from London," she said. "How would I ever get back to where I belong?"

Where did Lily belong? If she were truly the next seer, shouldn't she have an inkling she belonged with his clan? His grandmother never seemed surprised by anything, but she'd had many years to hone her gift.

"Merchant ships visit from time to time," he said. "Once the winter storms are past, it will not be difficult to find a ship to take ye to London."

Lily was quiet for a long moment. He wondered why she was so torn, when going with him was clearly the safer choice. But she was a stubborn lass who wanted to believe she could take care of herself. And perhaps she could in London. But not here.

"This place—this island—where you want to take me," she finally said, "is that where you live?"

"Nay, but I'll stay through Yuletide to see that you're settled," he said. "Then I must return to my duties on the Isle of Skye."

Ach, the lass looked relieved to hear it. That was a blow to his pride. And yet he did not believe the fire between them was kindled all on his side. If all Lily wanted was a night of passion with no further entanglement, he ought to be relieved.

The fact that he was not annoyed the hell out of him.

***

"Come to Islay," Roderick said. "Ye don't want to spend Yuletide alone."

"I usually do," she said. "I prefer it that way."

"Ye don't spend it with your family?" He sounded startled.

"I avoid them as much as I can—especially on feast days," she said. "My brothers, father, and uncles use any occasion as an excuse to get drunk and into fights, and they're always asking to borrow money."

Lily did not know why she was telling him about her family. She never spoke of them with anyone else.

"After I was apprenticed to the old healer, she and I enjoyed a quiet Christmas, lighting an extra candle and hanging greens in the shop," she said, smiling at the memory. "We sold bits of mistletoe and holly all through Advent."

Lily still sold mistletoe and hung greens during Advent, but she missed the old woman.

"Have ye no mother?" Roderick asked in a quiet voice.

"She died when I was a babe."

"My parents' boat was lost in a winter storm when I was a wee bairn, so I know something of your loss." He enfolded her hand in his. "But I've always had my grandmother and my clan."

35

Most of the time, Lily did not mind having no one to share feast days with. But on Christmas, she would take out all the old letters from her sister, who lived with her husband in France, and from her friend Linnet in Northumberland.

"Lily," Roderick said, drawing her attention back to the present. "I don't believe I can leave ye in Ayr."

"Why not?" Her heart beat fast at the thought, unlikely as it was, that he wanted to be with her a little longer.

"'Tis not safe for ye to be on your own in Ayr," he said. "I'd worry about ye there."

She was so unaccustomed to being worried about that his words made her eyes sting. When she was only a young child, her family had even moved to a different house without noticing they had left her behind until someone told them hours later.

"I may not do well in the wilderness," Lily told him, "but I can manage the dangers of a town."

"Nay, I'll not take ye there and leave ye," he said, shaking his head. "'Tis no use arguing. I've made up my mind."

Now he was being high-handed. "That's a shame, because I've made up my mind to go. I can walk the rest of the way."

"Ye must trust me on this, lass," he said, squeezing her hand. "Ye don't know this country, and ye can't speak our language."

She hated letting someone else make decisions for her. But, truth be told, Roderick had held her fate in his hands from the moment he rescued her on that barren hillside.

"With your sense of direction," he added, "you'd never get to Ayr anyway."

She laughed in spite of herself. "I'd wager all that talk about your grand Yuletide celebrations was just to persuade me to come with you."

"Aye," he said, a smile playing at the corners of his mouth. "But what I said about the mountains of food, great bonfires, and long tales is all true."

Lily could not muster any anger over his attempt to control her, since his only purpose was to keep her safe.

"My grandmother will be on Islay all winter," he said. "Ye can stay with her, and she'll teach ye those new cures you're wanting to learn."

36

She remembered hearing rumors that old magic, long forgotten in England, was still practiced in the wildest parts of Scotland. The prospect of learning these ancient skills sent a thrill through her.

"You'd do that for me?" she said. "Ask your grandmother to take me in?"

"It would be a favor to me," he said, resting his hand over his heart. "She's an old woman, and I don't like her to be alone. And there's bound to be more folk in need of healing at the Yuletide gathering than my old grandmother can manage on her own."

A kind man was as rare as a flea-less dog. Roderick's concern for both her and his grandmother touched Lily deeply, and it only added to his already formidable appeal.

She should get on her feet and start walking to Ayr before it was too late for a cure. But the night was dark and cold.

And Lily did not want to be cured just yet.

CHAPTER 6

Roderick stopped breathing as she reached out to him. When her fingertip touched his chest, he felt it all the way to the soles of his feet.

"Is that dried blood?" she said in an accusing tone as she stepped closer and narrowed her eyes at the tear in his tunic.

This was not what he was hoping for.

"I didn't notice it before against your dark tunic," she said. "Why did you not tell me you were hurt?"

"'Tis nothing," he said. "Harold grazed me as I knocked him to the ground."

"Take that off," she said.

From the determined way Lily was pushing up her sleeves, she was not suggesting they roll around on the grass naked.

"I've herbs in my bag to make a salve for it." She marched off into the darkness to retrieve her bag, which was a few yards away with the saddle.

Roderick sighed and pulled his tunic and shirt over his head. When she reappeared in the firelight a few moments later, he had the small satisfaction of watching her come to an abrupt halt and flush pink as she took a long look at his bare chest. She recovered quickly, however.

She sat down in front of him and poured some of his good whisky onto a cloth. "This will sting."

"You're making a lot of fuss over a wee scratch." He winced as she began cleaning his wound with the cloth.

"'Tis no *wee scratch*." She paused to fix him with a hard look. "An untended wound can turn feverish."

He leaned back on his elbow and watched as she mixed some powder from a vial into his eating bowl with a few more drops of his whisky to create a paste.

When she turned her attention back to him, he swallowed as her gaze drifted across his chest and arms, seeming to take in every inch of bared skin. Did she have any notion what that did to him?

"I see this is not the first time you've gotten yourself injured," she said, sounding irritated. "I suppose battle scars are a badge of honor for you Highlanders."

He shrugged. "Every scar provides a tale to share around the hearth."

"You should be more careful," she scolded.

"I am careful," he said with a laugh. "That's why I lived to tell the tales."

She blew out an exasperated breath, but a smile tugged at the corners of her pretty mouth.

Roderick tried to keep his thoughts from straying when she edged closer, but he utterly failed when her thigh rested against his and she leaned across him to apply the salve along the narrow line of the wound. His cock was already throbbing when her hair fell over her shoulder and brushed his belly just above his breeks.

Despite the chill in the air, he was beginning to sweat, but Lily was so focused on her task that she did not appear to notice his state. It was a small cut—would she never finish?

Jesu. With every stroke of her finger, the ends of her hair brushed his skin like a tantalizing invitation.

At last, she finished applying the salve. He expected her to move away from him at once. When she remained where she was, he dared to hope.

***

The tension between them was so strong it prickled Lily's skin. When she finally forced herself to look up, the fierce desire in Roderick's eyes stole her breath away. His dark blue gaze held her fast with a question. *Will you?*

This sinfully handsome Highlander did not need a woman to cook and clean or do the other things men expected. There was only one thing he wanted from a woman. And to Lily's everlasting surprise, he appeared to want it from her tonight.

She had avoided entanglements with men like the plague she knew them to be. She loved her shop and her freedom. Living a celibate life had been no great sacrifice. In truth, she had not met a single man who tempted her.

Until now. And by the heavens, she was sorely tempted.

Tomorrow they would be on their way, and soon after they reached Islay, she would never see Roderick again. If she was ever going to go to have a night of sinful pleasure with a man, she would never have a more suitable opportunity.

Nor a man she would rather do it with.

Roderick reached out and cupped her face with his hand. His touch was gentle, yet the effect on her was so powerful that she felt it to her toes. She already felt over her head and drowning. Perhaps she should wait and do this with some quiet, unassuming merchant who did not make her heart race and her limbs feel weak.

"Tell me more about your grandmother, the healer," she said to buy time to calm herself.

"I can't do that now." He took the bowl of salve Lily still had gripped in her hands without realizing it and set it by the fire.

"Why not?" she asked in a whisper.

"Because I may not survive," Roderick said, resting his hand on the small of her back, "if I wait any longer to kiss ye."

As he leaned toward her, her pulse skittered, and she could not get enough air. She recognized these as signs of a woman losing her wits over a man. She had often prepared soothing drinks for women who came to her breathless and agitated.

"Tell me ye want to kiss me," he said in a husky voice that vibrated inside her.

"I do," she said, desire overwhelming her good sense.

Mercy! The moment their lips touched, she was glad she was sitting, for her limbs went weak as she melted into his first soft, warm kiss.

Of course, she had been kissed before—by the stonemason's apprentice who nearly broke her tooth, the butcher's son who slobbered, and the occasional customer who managed to grab her before she kneed his groin. But none of those kisses bore any resemblance to this.

When Roderick ran his tongue along her bottom lip, she opened her mouth with a sigh. His tongue was slow and sensuous as he explored her mouth, but before long their kisses grew so heated that she had to pull away to catch her breath.

When she did, he covered her face in kisses—her cheeks, her brow, her eyelids, her hair. *Heavens*, it felt wondrous. He rested his hand on her ribs, where it touched the underside of her breast—*oh my*—while his lips traced a burning trail down the side of her throat. She did not remember lying down, but she was on her back.

40

While his kisses were gentle, coaxing, his shaft was hard against her belly. This Highlander was danger and mystery beneath a beguiling surface.

"I want ye so badly, lass," he said, his breath hot on her skin. "Say ye want me too."

When she did not answer, he leaned back and fixed his gaze on her face. She had to turn her head to the side to give herself a chance to think.

Since they soon would be parted forever, she need not worry about suffering through the deceit and lies, the other women, the endless demands, and all the other abuses men heaped upon women. She could enjoy one magical night that she could remember for the rest of her life, with none of the bad memories that usually followed.

And even more than that, she did not want her only time with a man to be that once when she had not been quick enough to get away from a man in her shop. He'd left with a long gash from her knife down his face that she hoped festered and killed him. When the old herbalist found her afterward, she gave Lily a tincture to prevent the rapist's seed from taking hold in her womb.

Lily had the herbs in her bag she would need to make that same tincture in the morning.

"We don't have to do this," Roderick said, but he kept his hands on her. "I'll leave ye alone if that's what ye want."

"I don't want you to leave me alone," she said, meeting his gaze. "I want this."

"Good."

She thought he would free the essential parts from their clothing, and be about the business of it quickly, as she'd often seen couples do against the wall in the backstreets of the city at night— and sometimes in the day. Instead, he got up on his knees.

He was so beautiful that she found herself staring at him, as she had when he first took off his shirt and tunic. Of course, she had known from riding with him for two days and watching him fight that he had a muscular frame, but that was not the same as seeing the hard, rippling muscles of his bared torso in the glow of the firelight.

"Aren't you cold?" she asked.

"Cold?" he said, raising an eyebrow. "Nay."

With that hunger in his eyes, she thought he would surely fall upon her now like the men who trapped her in corners and pawed at her until she jabbed her knee into their groin or pulled her knife. But he surprised her again by crouching at her feet.

She rose up on her elbows and watched him remove her boots. After the boots, he pulled off one of her wool stockings, and then he grinned at her as he cradled her bare foot in his hand.

"I knew I'd find a lass under here." He kissed the bottom of her foot with soft lips, and the scratch of his unshaven beard tickled and sent a thrill of tingles up her leg.

"I'm going to freeze without them," she said, when he pulled off her other stocking.

"I'll keep ye warm," he said, a wicked promise in his eyes.

She sucked in her breath as he slid his hand up her calf inside the lad's breeches she wore.

"I've been longing to touch your skin," he said. "And I've been imagining what ye feel like under the lad's clothes since I first found ye and your cap fell off."

"That long?" she asked, her voice coming out high.

"And every moment since." His gaze sizzled with heat as he lifted her hand and pressed a warm kiss to her palm.

After he lay down beside her and spread the blanket over them, his big hand came to rest on her hip. He was so gentle as he kissed her cheek and hair and said her name that she relaxed and enjoyed both the kisses and the sensation of his hard body against her side.

Still, a wave of uneasiness swept over her when Roderick pulled her tunic up, revealing a few inches of bare skin. Would he be disappointed? No doubt he had bedded many women who were beautiful—and who knew what they were doing and how to please him.

She was too distracted to hold on to that worry for long. He captured all her attention as he leaned over, kissed her bared belly, and ran his hands up her sides beneath the tunic. When he brushed the sides of her breasts, she sucked in her breath. A moment later, she forgot to breathe altogether as he slowly kissed his way up to her chest, easing the tunic up as he went.

"By the saints, lass, ye feel good," he murmured against her skin when he finally covered her breasts with his big, warm hands.

She nearly rose off the ground when he began to fondle her nipples, rolling them between his thumbs and fingers. *Good heavens,* she had no notion that would be so…arousing. Sensations thrummed through her and pooled in her belly and between her legs.

When he replaced his hand on one of her breasts with his mouth, she ceased to think at all. His tongue circled and flicked, teasing her nipple. Then he sucked it into his mouth, drawing tendrils of pleasure that were almost painful all the way from her toes. He moved to her other breast, and she thought she might go mad.

When he stopped and lay beside her again, she nearly groaned aloud in disappointment.

The firelight glinted in his hair and played over his handsome features as he watched her with his head propped on one elbow. "I want to take this slowly."

He slipped his hand under her tunic and ran a finger along the top of her breeches. How did such a light touch across her stomach, of all places, feel so delightfully wicked?

Their eyes locked as he slid the flat of his hand across her belly, then dipped his fingers beneath the top of her breeches. He paused, his heated gaze never leaving her face, as if waiting for her to object. Her breathing grew shallow as his hand began to inch downward. Her nipples were so sensitive she was aware of the rough cloth rubbing against them with every slight movement.

Her body jerked when he slid his fingers between her legs. She clenched her fist in the blanket. *Good God*, her Highlander had magic in his fingers. As he worked that magic, he kissed her throat and face and—*heaven help her*—her breasts. She made a weak attempt to stop making incoherent murmurs and moans like a madwoman.

"Ach, I love the sounds ye make," he said.

Her head was already spinning when she pulled him into a deep kiss. She ran her hands over his chest, into his hair, down his arms, and over his backside. She felt drunk on passion and could not touch him enough. Closer, she wanted him closer still.

He moved down her body until he pressed his lips to the bare skin just above her breeches. *Oh, Lord*, he was easing them down. Another inch, and he ran his tongue low across her belly between her hips. She felt breathless and on edge as he slowly drew the breeches down all the way to her knees.

43

He sat up and tugged them the rest of the way off her legs, then he covered her with his body. Their kisses, hungry and deep, went on forever. And all the while, his hands moved over her, exploring, prodding, caressing, as if he needed to touch every inch of her. When he cupped her breast and squeezed her nipple, she groaned into his mouth and arched her back.

"Tell me my torture is over," he gasped between kisses. "I must have ye. I must."

Tension thrummed through her body, and she dug her fingers into his shoulders to pull him closer. And still, she could not get as close as she wanted. His cock was pressing against the place that throbbed between her legs. While it felt *so* good, it made the fever raging inside her worse.

"I need to be inside ye," Roderick said, his voice strained. "Now. Please. Now."

Her mind was so addled with passion that she was slow to realize what was about to happen. Before she could prepare herself, she felt him start to penetrate her. He was too big. Panic seized her.

"You're so tight," he said, his voice desperate in her ear.

Tight? Was that good or bad? Before she could guess which, he thrust deep inside her. Her breath came out in a *whoosh*, and she stiffened, startled by a rush of sensation.

She was mortified when she had to bite her lip against a sudden threat of tears. Having him inside her, being joined with him like this, set loose an unexpected wellspring of emotions.

"Lily." Roderick went utterly still above her. Tension radiated from his body. "What is wrong?"

"Nothing," she said.

Roderick smoothed her hair from her face and gently kissed her forehead, which only made it worse. Feeling too exposed and vulnerable to look at him, she turned her face to the side.
He gently turned it back toward him again. His eyes were full of concern as they searched her face.

"Ach, did I hurt ye?" he said, and wiped a traitorous tear that slipped down her cheek.

"Truly, I'm fine," she said. "You needn't stop."

"I can't do this when 'tis plain ye regret it," he said, and started to ease out of her.

Was she to come this far for *naught?*

44

"I don't regret it," she said, grabbing his shoulders. "I said I want to do this, and I do."

"Are ye certain?" he asked, still looking uneasy.

"I couldn't bear it if you left me like this," she said. "I want to know how it ends."

"How it ends?" he asked, drawing his brows together.

"How it *ought* to be," she said, feeling impatient with him now. Why could he not just get on with it instead of making her explain? "I've only done it once, and..."

She did not want to talk about that other time, not now. Not ever.

"I take it that experience wasn't all a lass might hope for..." he said, raising an eyebrow. "Like a tale with a disappointing ending?"

"'Twas worse than disappointing."

His worried expression melted, and he laughed. For a frantic moment, she feared she had ruined everything. But then he held her face between his hands and gazed down at her with warmth in his eyes.

"I'll do my best to give this tale of ours a satisfying ending, *m' eudail,*" he said as he closed the short distance between their lips.

His kiss began warm and slow, and all the while she was keenly aware of every inch of his shaft inside her. When she instinctively lifted her hips, he groaned, and his shaft pulsed inside her.

Very slowly, he began moving inside her. His mouth was hot on hers, his tongue mimicking his slow, deep thrusts. She gave a soft moan of complaint when he pulled out nearly all the way, then gasped at the rush of pleasure when he thrust inside her again.

"*Mo leannain*, did I hurt ye again?" he asked.

She felt too much to speak, so she answered him by wrapping her arms around his neck and pulling him into another deep kiss.

His hand slid up her side and cupped her breast. When he rolled her nipple between his thumb and finger, bright sparks of pleasure shot through her. He was moving inside her, setting off sensations that were so intense she could hardly bear it.

Murmuring words in Gaelic to her, he kissed the side of her face, her hair, her throat. Then his tongue was in her ear, and she never would have guessed that would feel so enticing.

45

All the while, he continued moving inside her, sliding in and out at an excruciatingly slow pace. Tension built inside her until she thought she might burst. Her skin felt too tight.

"Lock your legs around me," he said in a strained voice.

When she did, he groaned as he slid deeper inside her.

"*Mo rùin*, I cannot go slowly much longer."

He was *trying* to go slow? She dug her nails into his arms.

"Please. I want... I want..." She could not form words for what she wanted.

But then he began moving faster, and all thought fled as her entire being was caught up in the movement of their bodies and the overwhelming sensations flooding through her. As his body rocked against hers, she held on to him with all her strength and met his thrusts, urging him harder, faster.

"Lily," he said, holding her face between his hands.

Their eyes locked as he thrust deep inside her. Her body clutched around his, and she cried out his name as waves of pleasure rolled through her.

Before she could catch her breath, he called her name again as he surged inside her, and she went over the edge with him.

***

Roderick lay awake watching the dark night clouds blowing across a blacker sky and wondering what in the hell had happened to him when they made love. He felt stunned, as if he had been struck in the head or something. He thought that surely the feeling would ease if they made love a second time. Yet he had felt just as stunned the second time. And the third.

She had only let a man take her to bed once before. Why did she choose him? Was it merely to satisfy her curiosity? Because she believed he would do a better job of it than the weak, fat-bellied merchants she knew in London?

He was still awake when the sky turned from black to gray, signaling the coming dawn. An opaque mist lay over the shore, obliterating their surroundings and making it seem as if there was no one but him and Lily in the world. He looked at her face as she slept in his arms, and his heart tripped a beat.

The utterly foolish idea of asking her to wed him flitted across his mind.

With his finger, he brushed a wild strand of flaming red hair from her cheek. She looked deceptively fragile, but she had such a strong spirit. He felt an overwhelming desire to protect her. Just because he succeeded in satisfying her in bed did not mean she wanted anything more from him.

How could he have let this wee elf of a lass, an English lass at that, grab hold of his heart?

Ach, last night was a mistake for so many reasons.

Before last night, he could have been content with a local lass from Skye who would count herself lucky to live near her kin and be satisfied with a strong husband who could protect her. Hoping for something more from a wife was a mistake. His first marriage should have taught him that.

As he watched Lily's eyelids flutter and her chest rise and fall with her shallow breathing in that dreamlike state between sleep and full wakefulness, he imagined watching her wake each morning. Before last night, he had not thought beyond delivering her to his clan. Now he was imagining a future he knew he could not have. And one she surely did not want.

His wife had found the isolation of the Isle of Skye unbearable, after growing up in the town of Inverness. How much harder would it be for a lass from the great city of London? And he would have to leave her alone for long periods of time. For a Highland warrior, there would always be battles to fight.

And he could not bear to make Lily unhappy.

CHAPTER 7

Lily opened her eyes to find Roderick staring at her intently. The memory of all that they had done during the night came back to her in a rush, making her cheeks go hot. She had never had such a magical experience or felt so close to another person.

"Good morning to ye," he said, and kissed her forehead.

Had he felt as much as she had? She was desperate to know and wondered what he would say to her. As the silence stretched between them, she felt as if a fist held her by the throat, making it impossible to swallow. She needed him to say something—that she was special, that he wished they could have more time together, at least that he enjoyed the night—anything but this silence.

"The fog is lifting," Roderick said, looking out toward the shore. "We should be on our way."

Without another word, he got up and put on his clothes, as if last night was just another night and she was just another woman. She felt as if she had been kicked in the stomach. If he had professed undying love, she would not have believed him any more than she had believed her merchant suitors. But all he could say to her after what had passed between them in the night was *The fog is lifting*?

Evidently, the night had not been utterly magical for him. After baring her soul—not to mention her body— it was painful to find she was so forgettable.

But she refused to be the sort of pathetic woman who would sniffle over a man. After pulling on her tunic, she furiously wiped her nose on the sleeve, then looked for the rest of her clothes under the blanket.

Where in the hell were her stockings?

Was her brave Highlander afraid to speak out of fear she expected an offer of marriage? He needn't have worried. The notion was ridiculous. She never wanted to be tied to a man who would tell her what to do and expect her to wash his clothes and fix his supper every night. And she knew as well as Roderick did that she did not belong here.

She had her shop in London, and she wanted to get back to it as soon as she could. The shop had always been her refuge.

It was all she had.

***

Roderick stomped to the nearby burn and splashed water on his face. Lily had her reasons for going to bed with him, but he did not believe that marriage was one of them.

He had not taken her virginity, so he was not honor-bound to wed her. And yet she had seemed so innocent that he almost felt as if he had been her first. Should he make the offer and tell her why she ought to refuse him? He doubted she would consider it anyway.

He was still debating what he ought to do when he returned to their camp and found Lily on her hands and knees, frantically searching the grass where their blanket had been.

"What is it, lass?" he asked, crouching beside her.

"'Tis gone!" she said, without looking up from her search. "I've lost it!"

He'd never seen her distressed like this before, though she'd had plenty of reason.

"I'll help," he said. "What are we looking for?"

"The key to my shop," she said in a choked voice.

He rested his hand on her shoulder. "Ye can always have a new lock and key made."

"I know." She sat down abruptly and turned her back to him, but not before he saw a tear slip down her cheek. "The door will be broken and everything stolen anyway."

"Then why is this key so important to ye?"

"'Tis a reminder of my old life," she said, "and a promise to myself that I'll be able to return to it one day soon."

Well, that made matters clear. The prospect of a marriage that would keep her in the Highlands forever would not be well received.

Since she had no feeling that she belonged here, it also seemed very doubtful that Lily was the seer his grandmother foretold. If she had *The Sight* at all, she hid it damned well. The key was lying right in front her in the grass.

"Here it is, lass," he said, and handed it to her.

"Praise God!" She clutched the key in her hands like a prayer and rested her head on her knees. "I don't belong here. I want to go home."

Her words left a hollow feeling in his chest. To comfort her, he sat beside her and put his arm around her.

"Well, ye can't go just yet," he said. "But in a few weeks, the winter storms will pass, and it will be safe to sail the open sea again."

By then, he'd know if she carried his child. If she did, he could give her no choice but to marry him. He did not know which made him feel worse—the thought of never seeing Lily again or the prospect of making a second wife miserable.

"You're a verra special lass," he said, squeezing her shoulders. "I'll hate to see ye go."

He was shocked to his boots when she turned and pulled him into a deep kiss. Soon, they were rolling on the ground lost in passion, with no thought of tomorrow.

CHAPTER 8

Lily gasped as another wave broke over the side of the boat, drenching her with cold spray. Her hair had blown free from its knot and whipped across her face, stinging her skin. Through the loose strands, she watched Roderick, fixing every image of him in her memory. She stifled a sigh and told herself not to ruin what little time she had left with him by dwelling on how miserable she would be when they parted.

Despite the rough sea, Roderick was laughing and talking with the other men as if he was unaware that the boat was bouncing like a cork. Clearly, the man was born to sail. After adjusting the ropes holding the sail, he crossed the boat to where she sat clinging to the bench to keep from sliding back and forth.

"'Tis a great day for sailing, aye?" he said with a wide grin.

Racing across the water was rather thrilling, but if she were honest with herself, she missed the physical closeness of riding on horseback with him. And she could do without the dozen other men in the boat, who eyed her while speaking in Gaelic.

"What are they saying?" she asked.

"Well, they're curious as to why I've returned with a Sassenach," he said. "But mostly, they're remarking on how fetching ye look in breeches."

She looked down at her wet and dirty clothes. *Fetching?* Either he was lying or these Highlanders had not seen a woman in a very long time. When they reached their destination, she would have to use one of her precious coins to buy a gown and shoes.

Roderick rested a hand on her shoulder and leaned down while he pointed to an island ahead. "That's the Isle of Islay, the center of the great MacDonald clan. We'll leave the galley in the bay and walk inland to Finnlaggan."

She heard reverence in his voice when he spoke of Finnlaggan, but she did not expect to be impressed. As a Londoner, she had seen royal processions, royal barges, and the formidable walls of the two royal palaces on the Thames.

"Clan MacDonald has castles throughout the isles and on the mainland," he said. "But Finnlaggan is where Alexander, the Lord of the Isles, meets with the council, and he considers it his home."

After the men pulled the boat onto the shore between dozens of others, Roderick lifted her down. The ground felt as if it were rolling under her like the sea, and she was grateful for Roderick's arm to steady her as they followed the others down a well-trod path.

They had walked some distance when they entered a large meadow with a lone holly tree on one side of the path and a tall, rectangular stone on the other.

"What is that stone?" she asked, pointing.

"'Tis from long, long ago, before our people were Christian, before the oldest tales of our heroes. You'll find stones like this alone and in circles throughout the Highlands. Some believe they still hold ancient magic."

Lily felt an odd vibration in the air, like the buzz of a bee's wings. It grew stronger as they neared the tall stone.

"I feel it," she blurted out.

Roderick halted and gave her a penetrating look. Unease crept up her spine.

"You don't think I'm a witch, do you?" she asked.

He crossed the path to the holly tree, snapped off a sprig, and stuck it in her hair. Then he winked at her. "Holly wards off evil. A witch cannot wear it."

"If the London rabble knew that," she said with a relieved laugh, "I could have worn holly and saved myself a long journey."

His expression turned serious again, and he took her hand. "What happened in London that made ye leave?"

She trusted him enough now to tell him. Roderick was a good man, and he would not turn on her.

"Witch fever was at a high pitch, and mobs were roaming the streets," she said. "I knew they would burn innocent women like me next. My heart told me I must leave, so I did."

"Ye need have no fear of that here," he said, and put his arms around her. "Women with your gift—healers—are valued by us Highlanders."

He stood in the middle of the path holding her and murmuring soothing Gaelic into her hair for a long time. Heaven help her, but she would miss him.

They held hands as they resumed their walk. Eventually, they crested a hill, and a large inland loch appeared nestled in the valley below. The village along the shore seemed to be a hive of activity, with people, carts, and horses. That looked promising. She should be able to ply her trade here.

Roderick drew her attention to the two islands in the loch. The larger one was connected to the shore by a narrow causeway and to the smaller island by a bridge.

"The small island farther from shore is *Eilean na Comhairle*, The Council Island," Roderick explained. "The single stone building on it is the meeting place for the Council of the Isles, which is comprised of the chieftains from the branches of the MacDonald clan and chieftains from the clan's vassals, including the MacLeods, Mackenzies, MacNeils, Macleans."

The Lord of the Isles apparently was a far grander person than she had reckoned. Roderick had not exaggerated when he said this chieftain of chieftains was like a king.

"I have business to attend to on the large island, Eilean Mor," he said. "It houses the Lord of the Isles' Great Hall, his family living quarters, guest quarters, and a chapel. The smaller buildings ye see with thatched roofs are for storage, workshops, and the like."

Lily's heart began to race as they walked along the shore of the loch toward the village. She tried to steel herself to part ways with Roderick. When they reached the causeway to the island, just outside the village, she halted.

"Before we say farewell, I want to tell you how grateful I am for all you've done for me." She had to pause to fight the tears stinging the back of her eyes. "You saved my life."

"Lily—" He started to speak but stepped when she held up her hand.

"I am grateful for the kindness you showed me and…for what we did last night." She dropped her gaze to her ugly boots and spat out the rest quickly. "You mentioned I might stay with your grandmother. Will I find her in the village? If not, I'm sure I can manage on my own here. Just as you said, this is a good place."

"I'm not leaving for Skye for a few days," he said, lifting her chin with his finger. "Are ye that anxious to be rid of me?"

She shook her head.

"We can explore the village later," he said, "but now we're going to have a fine meal in the Great Hall while I wait to speak with my chieftain."

"Me? Eat in the Great Hall?" She was just a lowly shopkeeper.

He looked her up and down. "Aye, we must find ye a gown in the village first."

Roderick proved as efficient at this as he was at everything else. When he saw a woman beating a rug outside her cottage, he asked her if she had a second gown she would sell for a silver coin. The woman recognized a good bargain when she heard one, and she proved to be both kind and Lily's size. A short time later, Lily emerged from the cottage wearing a faded but clean blue gown. She had also washed her face and attempted to tidy her unruly hair.

"Ach, ye look lovely," Roderick said, taking her in from head to toe and back again.

Another lie, to be sure, but she did feel less conspicuous out of the breeches.

The sun was low in the winter sky by the time they crossed the causeway and reached the island, which was overflowing with people and activity. They had to step aside to make way for several carts and horses.

"Is it always like this?" she asked.

"It is whenever the Lord of the Isles is in residence," he said. "Alexander is celebrating the Yuletide here."

The guards who stood outside the doors of the Great Hall greeted Roderick with deference, confirming her growing suspicion that this Highlander, whom she had first taken for a wild heathen, was highborn and far above her station. It made her uneasy.

They entered a huge room that must be thirty by sixty feet long, with a roaring fire in a massive stone hearth. She tilted her head back to take in the high ceiling—then belatedly closed her gaping mouth. Despite what Roderick had told her about the Lord of Isles, she had expected his Great Hall to be more on a par with a well-to-do cloth merchant's home in London. She had never seen such fine furnishings and rich tapestries.

The meal had already begun, and the room was noisy with a hundred conversations. The long tables were loaded with platters of food of all sorts, and servants were still bringing more.

54

Jewels sparkled on both men and women. Most of the men wore Highland garb like Roderick's, but there was a sprinkling who looked to be wealthy Flemish, French, and English merchants. The women, except for those who were obviously servants, were dressed like English noblewomen in elaborate headdresses and fine velvet and linen gowns.

Lily's eyes were drawn to the high table and a tall, golden-haired man with a hawk nose and commanding presence who sat at the center seat. This must be Alexander, the Lord of the Isles, himself. Her imagination got the better of her. Despite the distance and the noisy roomful of people between them, she felt for a moment as if his piercing eyes were fixed on her.

She held fast to Roderick's arm. As they passed one of the long trestle tables, men nodded or called out to him and women followed him with their eyes. He found room for them at the end of another table, but before they could sit, one of the guards tapped Roderick on the shoulder and spoke to him in Gaelic.

Lily assumed the guard was telling him the seats were taken and they must leave. Closing her eyes, she breathed in the delicious aromas from the heaping platters of food. She would feel more comfortable eating with the servants in the kitchen, if that were permitted, but she dearly wanted to eat.

"We're invited to sup at the high table," Roderick said, leaning down so she could hear him over the voices and clatter.

Lily's pulse leaped. Nobles occasionally came to her shop when they had ailments they did not wish to disclose even to their servants, but she had never been inside such a fine hall before, let alone eaten at a high table.

"Must we?" she asked.

"Aye," he said, and squeezed her hand. "This is my clan. You've nothing to fear here."

Lily took a deep breath and let Roderick lead her past all the other tables. He held her hand, which made her heart flutter and earned her more than a few frowns and arched brows.

She had expected him to treat her as a mere fellow traveler. After all, they were parting ways here on the Isle of Islay. Instead, he appeared to be proclaiming to his kin that she was something more to him. He glared at the men who stared at them, as if in warning.

Why was he sending them the message that she belonged to him? Was it simply to protect her?

Once they were settled near the end of the high table, Lily glanced around at the elaborate dishes and delicacies. She did not know what half of them were. The one with the pig's head was obviously pork, and she recognized the oysters, beef, lamb, honeyed nuts, and cheeses, but none of those were within reach.

The platter closest to her had some sort of roasted meat decorated with a splay of feathers in dazzling colors.

"What is that?" she whispered to Roderick.

"You've never eaten peacock?" he asked with a wink, and dished a large helping onto the trencher they shared. "'Tis verra tasty."

As she stuffed herself with one new delicious dish after another and shared a cup with Roderick, she surreptitiously examined the wicked-looking weapons on the walls and her dinner companions at the table. These Highlanders were not primitive heathens, as she had heard back in London. And yet there was a wildness about them, to be sure. Roderick looked as intimidating as any of them, but she had grown accustomed to him.

And seen him naked. She blushed and took another gulp of wine to hide her smile. Luckily, Roderick had been drawn into conversation—in Gaelic—with some of the other men at the table.

When the man on her other side cleared his throat, she turned and gave him a polite smile. He had a touch of gray in his hair, flashing dark eyes, and he wore the most beautifully made tunic she had ever seen. It even had tiny jewels sewn onto it.

"*Parlez-vous Français?*" he asked. "Or English, perhaps?"

"I do!" she said. "I'm a Londoner."

She was relieved to have someone she could speak with at the table. When she found out he was a merchant who had come to Islay in his own ship, her heart beat fast. Perhaps she would not have to wait here through the long winter after all.

"I should have sailed home to Spain already," he said, and sipped his wine. "The winter here is beastly. I intend to set sail on the morrow."

"How far is Spain from London?"

56

"A very long way, my dear," he said, his eyes sparkling with amusement. "But I'm stopping in London on my way. I have business in that dreary city before I return home to Spain."

By the time his ship reached London, it should be safe for her to return. She looked at Roderick, who was in deep discussion with his clansmen. If she left tomorrow, she would miss a day or two with him before his own departure. But it would be nothing like when they traveled alone. Roderick was an important man here and would have little time for her.

"What about the winter storms?" she asked.

"I have a large, sturdy ship," he said. "I've made the trip with her many a time."

"Could you take me with you?" she asked. "I have coin to pay my way."

"I don't need your coin, but I'd be delighted to have your company." He raised his eyebrows and nodded toward Roderick. "Provided your Highlander has no objection…"

"He's not my Highlander," she said. "And he's leaving here soon himself."

"All the same, I suspect he wouldn't take it well," he said with another glance at Roderick. Then he waggled his eyebrows and added, "But if you wish to come, I sail at daybreak."

CHAPTER 9

Where was his grandmother? As clan seer, she held a revered position and would be seated at the high table if she were in the hall. Most likely she had simply retired early, but Roderick was anxious about her. Fortunately, his twin cousins, Angus and Ian, who were tasked with bringing her to Islay, were seated next to him.

"Who's the bonny Sassenach?" Angus asked as he leaned forward and tried to catch Lily's eye.

"Ach, I like a fiery redhead," Ian said. "Aren't ye going to introduce us?"

The twins were nineteen, an age when they were full of themselves, and they received far too much encouragement from the lasses.

"Nay, I'll not introduce ye. And you're not to go near her." Roderick glared at them until they nodded. "Now tell me, is Seanmhair well?"

"She looked same as always last we saw her," Angus said as he stabbed a hunk of roasted pork from a platter.

"Have neither of ye seen fit to look in on her since ye brought her here?" Roderick wanted to grab the pair and knock their heads together.

"We couldn't," Ian said, and took a long drink of his ale, irritating Roderick further.

"Which guest chamber is she in?" He intended to find her as soon as the meal was finished.

"She's not," Angus said.

"Not what?"

"Not here."

"She wouldn't come with us," Ian put in. "Ye know how she is."

"So ye left her on Skye?"

"She claimed *The Sight* told her not to come," Angus said, rolling his eyes. "Ye know verra well, Roderick, that if Seanmhair doesn't want to do a thing, she doesn't."

That was true enough. And she was not above claiming *The Sight* told her not to come when it was just her own stubbornness. What was he going to do with Lily now? He'd told her she could stay with his grandmother, and he'd counted on them looking after each other after he left Islay.

He turned his attention back to Lily and saw that the slippery Spaniard in the ostentatious tunic was attempting to charm her. And the man appeared to be succeeding.

Before he could do more than glare at the Spaniard, one of Alexander's elite personal guards appeared behind him and tapped him on the shoulder.

"The lord wishes to speak with ye in private late tonight," the guard said next to Roderick's ear. "I'll find ye at the bonfire when he wants ye."

Roderick nodded. Since Alexander did not want to see him for a few hours, he could make good on at least one of the promises he'd made to Lily.

Alexander had just left the table, signaling the Yule bonfire would be lit soon.

"Tonight is the first night of Yuletide," Roderick said to Lily, interrupting the too-quiet conversation she was having with the Spaniard, and held out his hand. "Come, I'll show ye how we MacDonalds celebrate."

He swept Lily away and headed for the doors. As everyone else was doing the same, he had to work his way through throngs of his clansmen, every last one of whom was burning to ask him about the red-haired Sassenach. He did not feel like explaining, so he nodded as he passed them and kept moving.

He was nearly to the doors when he heard his former wife's voice behind him.

"Roderick!"

What in hell did Maigrid want? Had she not humiliated him enough? Ignoring her was pointless. Nonetheless, he tried.

"Roderick!" she called again, and this time she caught hold of his arm.

He cursed under his breath before turning around. Maigrid was as beautiful as ever, but the effect was lost on him now.

"Will ye be staying here on Islay long?" She paused and touched his sleeve. "I've missed ye, Roderick."

THE GIFT: A Highland Novella

There was only one thing she missed about him. But if she thought he was going to slip away with her for a night under the blankets, she was sadly mistaken. He made that mistake once after she left him, thinking she meant to return.

Ach, he was annoyed with himself for blaming her. He should have known better.

***

Lily felt like a squat toad next to the tall, stunning woman with golden hair, large hazel eyes, and a bright smile aimed at Roderick.

The woman held out her hands to him, which he pointedly ignored. Undeterred, she ran fingers down his arm as she spoke to him in Gaelic in a light, musical voice.

She looked at Roderick as if she'd like him on a platter with a honey glaze she could lick off. The two obviously knew each other intimately. Judging from Roderick's reaction, Lily had a good idea who this tall beauty was.

When the woman moved to place herself between Lily and Roderick, Lily started to step back, but Roderick held her arm in an iron grip.

"Ye must excuse us, Maigrid," he said in English. "I don't want my guest to miss the lighting of the bonfire."

He gave the woman a curt nod, then cut through the crowd, taking Lily with him.

Apparently when Roderick was done with a woman, he was done. Still, it was obvious this Maigrid had wounded him deeply. Lily wanted to go back and slap her for hurting him. At the same time, she felt pathetic for wishing he felt half that strongly for her.

"That was her, wasn't it?" Lily whispered after they were outside and some distance from the Great Hall. "The one who left ye while your enemy had ye chained in a dungeon?"

Roderick trained his eyes straight ahead and kept walking, which was answer enough.

"She is beautiful."

"Hmmph."

"I have a vial of poison in my bag…"

Roderick snorted and squeezed her shoulders. Lily was only half joking, but she was glad she had lifted his sour mood.

"Ye do know how to make me laugh," he said. "But there's no need to poison Maigrid. She doesn't matter anymore."

Ha.

"I doubt poison would work on her anyway," Lily said, which made him laugh again. "Ye can't poison a snake."

The woman probably could not wear holly either.

***

They followed the crowd across the causeway to a wide, open area on the shore of the loch where there was an enormous pile of wood four times her height. The sky was pitch black and a cold wind blew across the island, making Lily shiver as they waited in the darkness with the crowd. After a time, she felt a ripple of anticipation rising from the people around her.

"Look." Roderick put his arm around her and pointed. "Here they come."

A procession of flaming torches appeared across the loch. Against the black night, nothing was visible except the torches and their refection in the water. They looked like balls of fire moving along the shoreline. Lily had never seen anything more beautiful.

When the torch carriers reached the gathering, they encircled the enormous pile of wood. Then they chanted in deep male voices that pulsed through her, and she sensed it was a chant from ancient times, marking the solstice.

She jumped as one of the men tossed his torch onto the woodpile, and it exploded in flame.

"There's grease on the wood," Roderick said with a laugh as he squeezed her shoulders again.

After the lighting of the bonfire, jugs of whisky came out and the crowd grew jovial. Lily had heard that the Christmas celebrations at court were a sight to behold—and enormously expensive—but she could not imagine those had the drama and exuberance of these Highlanders' Yuletide celebrations.

The enormous bonfire crackled and spit, shooting flames high into the sky and making the front of her clothing hot to the touch. Everywhere she looked, laughter shone on the faces in the firelight. Roderick took a pull from a jug his neighbor handed him, then passed it on to her.

"You're not accustomed to it," he said. "Best take just a wee nip."

"Is that a challenge?" she asked. "I'll have ye know, I come from a long line of drunkards. 'Tis like mother's milk to me."

She leaned her head back and took a big gulp. Fire burned her throat and shot down her limbs, and she coughed and hacked until her eyes watered. Roderick thumped her on the back and laughed.

The sounds of a drum, flute, and an instrument she'd never heard before filled the air.

"Come, the dancing is about to begin," Roderick said, grabbing her hand.

"I don't dance."

If he heard her objection over the noisy celebrations, he blithely ignored it.

Suddenly they were part of a large circle of people moving first left and then right around the bonfire as they shouted a song. Though the steps to the dance were more elaborate, Lily found she could keep up by simply stepping sideways with the music. Unexpected laughter bubbled up inside her as she danced.

Through the din she heard Roderick's deep and rich voice singing with the others. When he squeezed her hand, she turned to find him grinning at her. He looked like a young and carefree man, not the hardened and ever-vigilant warrior who brought her across half of Scotland. Being with his clan brought him joy. She wondered what it would be like to feel so bonded with the people one lived amongst.

She was breathless and thirsty when they finally left the circle. The whisky slid down far more easily the second and third times and went to her head.

Through the crowd, she caught a glimpse of the Spaniard. If she was sailing with him, she must rise early and walk to the bay before dawn. Her spirits plummeted at the thought. But as much as she had enjoyed this night, she did not want to remain here without Roderick. These were not her people.

"Are ye all right?" Roderick asked over the boisterous singing.

"I'm tired. I should go to bed," she said, and then realized they had never found his grandmother. "Where am I to sleep?"

"For now, you'll be in one of the guest chambers with some other lasses," he said. "I'll take ye there now."

With everyone else at the bonfire, it was quiet on the walk back. Lily tried to sort out her feelings and decide whether to board the Spaniard's ship in the morning. This was likely the last opportunity she'd have to leave for weeks and weeks. It would be foolish not to take it, and yet...

Roderick led her past the Great Hall to a two-story stone building. Once inside, he led her up a set of stairs lit by torches fixed in the wall sconces.

"Here it is," he said, opening a heavy wooden door with an iron latch and hinges.

The bedchamber was glaringly empty, an open invitation. The tension grew taut between them as they stood in the doorway looking at the large bed. It was not difficult to read Roderick's thoughts when he turned toward her. They were the same as hers.

"I'd wager that the other lasses who share your chamber will be at the bonfire until dawn," he said, his gaze burning into her.

She could not risk missing that boat. Yet she could not let Roderick go quite yet. She rested her palms against his chest and closed her eyes. How could she say no to him when she would never see him again? Was one night worth what it would cost her?

"One kiss," she said, rising on her toes. "One kiss. Then you must go."

***

One kiss would not be nearly enough, but Roderick would take whatever she would give.

He leaned down, intending just to brush her lips. But at the soft touch, his heart lurched, and he pulled her against him. She gave a soft moan, and her arms went around his neck as they deepened the kiss.

He could not have said how long they stood kissing in the doorway as if they'd never have the chance again. When she pulled away, he watched her face in the torchlight, hoping to see the desire he felt reflected in their deep green pools.

"One night *is* worth it," she murmured as she brushed her fingertips across his cheek. "It is."

He was not sure what she meant, but it sounded promising. He glanced at the bed inside the room, then back at her, hoping she'd say aye.

"Roderick!"

He turned to see the guard who had spoken to him earlier about meeting with Alexander. *Damn it.*

"I've been looking all over for ye," the guard said as he climbed the stairs. His gaze shifted to Lily, then back to Roderick. "The Lord of the Isles wishes to see ye now."

Ach, why did the guard have to find him? If it were anyone else but the Lord of the Isles who wanted him, Roderick would make him wait.

"Let me bid the lass goodnight," Roderick said, glaring at the guard, then he leaned down and spoke in Lily's ear. "Shall I come back afterward?"

Before she had a chance to answer, the guard spoke again. "The lord says to bring the Sassenach with ye."

CHAPTER 10

What reason could Alexander have for inviting Lily to their private conference? Roderick did not like it. He glanced at Lily as they followed the guard. She looked far too fetching in that gown. Though it was simple, the color showed off her red hair, and it did not hide her womanly shape.

He wished he had left her dressed as a lad.

Most chieftains had numerous women—wives, mistresses, and occasional bedmates. Alexander, however, had set aside his "church wife" to wed a woman whose beauty would long be remembered in song, and by all accounts he was devoted to her. He had even ignored an edict from the Pope to cease cohabiting with her and return to his church wife.

But Alexander's wife was not on the Isle of Islay tonight.

A short time later, they stood before the door to the Lord of the Isles' private solar.

"Say *nothing*," Roderick hissed at Lily as the guards opened the door.

"How did ye find the Douglas chieftain?" Alexander asked after they exchanged formal greetings.

"Just as I expected," Roderick said. "Conniving and untrustworthy."

Alexander chuckled. "I'll not trust him either, cousin, except when our interests coincide."

"The Douglas gave me a reply to carry back to you," Roderick said, and waited for his chieftain to signal for him to approach. The warrior who always stood guard behind the chieftain's chair knew Roderick's loyalty, but protocols that served to protect the Lord of the Isles must be followed.

"I'll have my scribe read it to me later," Alexander said, and passed the missive to his clerk, a tall, stoop-shouldered man in churchman's robes who stood unobtrusively to one side.

Roderick was a trifle annoyed that his chieftain showed so little interest in a message he had traveled across the Lowlands to bring to him.

"Your grandmother told me that the Douglas chieftain would propose I join him in rebellion against the crown," Alexander said. "He suggests we ally ourselves with the English."

"The English!" Roderick was about to give his chieftain his opinion in a string of curses, but he stopped short when he realized Alexander had turned his gaze on Lily.

"I can use his message against him should I need it." Alexander dismissed the traitorous proposal with a wave of his hand and leaned forward. "So this is the lass."

"My lord?" Roderick asked, with a sense of impending doom.

"The one your grandmother foretold."

His grandmother had told Alexander? Roderick started to sweat. "My grandmother often speaks in riddles. Who knows what she meant?"

"She told me quite plainly that if I sent ye, you'd return with a lass," the chieftain said. "And so ye have."

Ach, he should have left Lily in the village.

"'Tis fortunate Roderick has brought ye to live among us," Alexander said, speaking directly to Lily. "The clan needs ye, lass, and I welcome ye as one of us."

Praise God Lily could not understand a word they were saying.

"What does he say?" she whispered, turning wide eyes on him.

"He welcomes ye," Roderick said. "That's the sum of it."

Lily gave Alexander a lovely smile and dipped a curtsey.

Alexander turned back to him. "Have ye made your pledges yet?"

The blood drained from Roderick's head. "Pledges?" he choked out. "Lily and me?"

"So ye haven't," the Lord said, narrowing his eyes at him. "I wish it to be done and soon."

"But why?" he said. "I was only to bring her back with me."

"Did your grandmother not tell ye that this lass must be bound to the clan through marriage?"

Roderick was too stunned to speak. What had his grandmother done?

"I can see that the old woman did not share that part of her vision with ye, which was probably wise on her part." Alexander gave a dry laugh. "All the same, ye shall wed the lass."

Lily elbowed Roderick's side. "I heard my name. What are ye saying about me?"

"Nothing," he hissed.

"'Twas apparent the moment ye entered the hall that ye had claimed her," Alexander said. "But taking her to your bed is not enough. According to your grandmother, ye must be bound in marriage."

"What are the two of you saying about me?" Lily asked in a louder whisper.

Before Roderick had time to invent something, the scribe moved to Lily's other side and spoke to her in a hushed voice.

"Roderick said he fulfilled his duty by bringing ye here," the scribe said in perfect English.

Roderick felt her stiffen beside him and prayed she would give him a chance to explain. He glared at the sallow clerk, willing him not to say the rest of it.

"And Alexander, Lord of the Isles, said that bringing ye here and taking ye to bed was insufficient," the clerk droned on in a low rumble. "Ye must be bound to him in marriage."

Lily went so pale Roderick feared she would faint. But when he took her arm to steady her, she gave him a fiery glare and shook him off.

***

Lily felt Roderick's gaze return to her again and again as the clerk continued translating the exchange between Roderick and the chieftain in a low undertone. Every word was another dart to her heart.

Roderick had used her and lied to her from the start.

She fixed her gaze on a shield that hung on the wall and concentrated on her breathing. In and out. In and out. Her skin felt stretched tight against the rising tide of violent emotions inside her until she could not remain in the room another moment, could not bear to hear one more word of his deceit.

When she turned to make her escape, the stern-faced guards stood in front of the door, blocking her way. Behind her, she heard the chieftain speak, and the guards stepped aside and swung the door open. As it closed behind her, Lily ran blindly, neither knowing nor caring where she went.

CHAPTER 11

"Lily! Lily, wait!"

She heard Roderick above the pounding of blood in her ears and ran faster. Her chest hurt as if were squeezed by a giant fist. She was desperate to get outside where she could breathe. She saw a door ahead and burst through it only to find herself in another torch-lit corridor.

Roderick caught her arm and spun her around.

"Let me explain," he said.

"No need," she said. "'Tis abundantly clear."

"Ye don't understand—"

"Your clan needed a seer, and ye thought I was one," she said. "Don't tell me more lies. That *is* why you brought me here."

She should have known he had not done it to protect her. What a fool she was. She had even begun to believe he cared for her.

"Did ye forget that ye were half dead when I found ye?" he said. "I brought ye with me because ye had nowhere else to go and no one to care for ye."

"And I'd still be lying on that hillside if your clan didn't need a seer."

"I didn't even know ye were a lass at first," he said. "How can ye believe I would have left ye there to die, no matter who ye were?"

"You could have left me in Ayr, but by then you'd convinced yourself I was this woman your grandmother foretold." She was so angry her vision blurred. "You invented an excuse, claiming the town wasn't safe."

"It wasn't safe."

"Nay." She swallowed. "You decided to do *whatever* you must to persuade me to come with you."

"It wasn't like that," he said.

"Yes, it was exactly like that," she said, choking out the words.

***

69

How had things gone so wrong? Roderick did not know what to do. God help him, Lily was on the verge of weeping.

"'Tis why you took me to bed," she said, pointing a finger at him.

"That was not the reason." Her accusation stung. Making love to her had affected him in ways he still did not understand. And yet a sliver of guilt niggled at him, making him feel lower than dirt. Though it had *not* been the reason, he had believed that making love to her would make her more amenable to continuing the journey with him.

"You pretended you wanted *me*." She shoved his chest with both hands, but tears were flowing down her cheeks. "You made me believe it!"

"I *did* want ye. I *do* want ye," he said, gripping her arms. "How can ye doubt it?"

He was in serious trouble. Lily was not the sort of lass who shed tears easily. Would she ever forgive him?

"I admit that I did wish to persuade ye to come here to Islay," he said. "But making love wasn't something I planned. It just happened. And I'm glad it did."

"Is that so, Highlander?" she said, putting her hand on her hip.

Ach, she was calling him Highlander. Not a good sign, but he preferred facing her anger over her tears.

"Well, ye troubled yourself for nothing," she continued. "I can't be that seer you're looking for because I don't have *The Sight*."

"Whether ye are a seer or no, I became responsible for ye when I saved your life," he said. "And when I took ye to bed, that changed everything."

"That changed nothing. You're not responsible for me. I don't belong to you," she said, poking his chest with each point she made. "And I'm not the woman you're looking for."

Was she saying that to dissuade him, or did she believe it?

"Ye cannot fight fate, lass," he said.

"If I had *The Sight*," she said, "I would have known not to walk to the border and risk dying on that hillside, now wouldn't I?"

"A seer cannot always see her own fate," he said, making it up as he went. "Have ye considered that ye were on that hillside because I was meant to find ye?"

Perhaps they were fated to be together.

She stared at him for a long moment, and he wondered if she shared the same thought. But then she spun away to face the wall, as if she could not stand to look at him. He watched her profile, illuminated in the glow of the torchlight.

"You're a thick-headed man," she said. "I want to go home."

Her declaration pierced him. Though she had been so frightened of the London mobs that she traveled hundreds of miles alone into a strange land to escape, she would rather return than be with him.

"I've told ye, 'tis too dangerous to sail the open sea with winter upon us."

"I don't care," she said, folding her arms. "I'm going anyway."

"The Lord of the Isles wishes ye to remain on MacDonald lands," he said. "No boat will take you away against his wishes."

When she squeezed her eyes shut and pounded her fist against the wall, he felt as if a giant hole had opened beneath him, and he was falling fast.

CHAPTER 12

"I'll take ye back to your chamber," Roderick said, gripping her elbow.

"Don't touch me." She jerked her arm away. "I don't need you to escort me. I remember the way."

"'Tis not safe for a lass to walk about on her own with drunken warriors everywhere."

She brushed away an angry tear. Arguing would be pointless, so she fixed her gaze ahead and marched down the corridor.

"In the morning after you're rested," he said, "we can discuss how to change the chieftain's mind and avoid this marriage, if that's what ye wish."

If that's what she wished? Was he daft? He had deceived her. It gave her no comfort that he, in turn, had been deceived. When she remembered the horror on his face upon learning that he was expected not just to deliver her but to wed her, Lily had to hold her breath to keep from weeping—which infuriated her all the more.

"Don't pretend you wish us to marry any more than I do," she snapped as she marched up the stairs to her guest chamber. "Though I expect your chieftain would reward you well for suffering with me as a wife."

There was no possibility she would let that happen.

When they reached the door, she was assaulted with the memory of the passionate kisses they had shared at this very spot an hour before.

"Give me time," he said. "I'll find a way to make this right."

She bit her lip as he brushed a stray tangle of hair from her cheek. Despite everything he'd done, she had to fight the temptation to lean against him and rest her head against his chest.

"Lily," he said, and rested his hand on the back of her waist, drawing her toward him.

For a moment, she was caught in the treacherous memory of how it had felt to be wrapped in his arms as he said her name and moved inside her. The enchantment he wielded on her was so strong that she wanted to believe he cared for her, that it had not all been a lie.

Before she weakened, she ran inside, slammed the door in his face, and threw the bar across. While he called her name and pounded on the other side, she leaned her back against the door and slid slowly to the floor.

***

Roderick sat in his guest chamber drinking far too much, though his celebratory mood was long gone.

He had a nagging feeling that he ought to go back to Lily's chamber. Each time it pulled at him, he took another drink and stifled the urge. When she slammed the door in his face, he had banged on it until his hand was bruised. It was the middle of the night now. She needed her sleep, and he should be sober when he tried to make amends to her.

Winning Lily's forgiveness would not be easy. And how in God's name was he going to mollify his chieftain when he refused to wed her? He sure as hell was not going to force Lily to be his wife.

He took another long drink.

He woke up with a start, dreaming he heard Lily call his name. Squinting against the daylight eking through the narrow window, he saw that he was still fully dressed, sprawled across the bed.

His throat was parched, his tongue felt like sand, and he had a blinding headache. He got up and splashed water on his face from the ewer. As he drank down a cup of stale ale he found on the table, he looked out the window.

Through the hills, he had a narrow view of the bay and the sea beyond. Something caught his eye—a dark red sail small as his thumbnail from this distance, disappearing over the horizon.

The Spaniard's ship. He remembered Lily and the Spaniard talking with their heads together during supper. Damn it, he knew it in his gut that she was on that ship. If she was, he would sail after it and fetch her.

He was strapping on his sword when a fist pounded at the door loud enough to make him wince. He swung open the door to find one of Alexander's personal guards.

"The Lord of Isles wants you," the guard said. "Now."

73

"There's something I must do first." Roderick was desperate to go to Lily's chamber in the hope of proving his instincts wrong. And if his instincts were right, he was going after her.

"Nay, ye must come at once," the guard said, shaking his head. "The chieftain is in a fury."

A few moments later, Roderick strode into Alexander's solar, fuming with impatience.

"Your Sassenach disappeared," Alexander greeted him.

Roderick's heart nearly stopped in his chest. Lily was gone. She must have left in the night, with drunken Highland warriors at every turn. Anything could have happened to her. She could be lying in a field, raped and bloody.

"Good God," he said, "I must find her."

"I sent men all over the island looking for her earlier," Alexander said with an icy glare, then he added through his teeth, "While you slept."

"She may have boarded that Spaniard's ship," Roderick said, anxious to be on his way. "I'll go after her."

"No need," Alexander said, drumming his fingers on the arm of his elaborately carved chair. "I already have her."

Praise God. Relief coursed through Roderick's limbs. "Where is she? Is she all right?"

Alexander slammed his fist on the arm of his chair and roared, "I'm not accustomed to being disobeyed!"

Roderick had been so worried about Lily that he had failed to appreciate that the Lord of the Isles was enraged.

"I honored that English lass by welcoming her to the great clan MacDonald, and I made clear my wish that the two of ye wed." Alexander got up and paced the room with his hand clenched around the jeweled hilt of the dirk at his belt. "Yet I must send warriors searching every path, every cottage, every boat, looking for the wretched lass."

"I understand Lily has tried your patience, but she's a Sassenach and doesn't understand our ways."

"She was found on the Spaniard's ship," he spat out, "dressed as a lad."

"Let me speak to her," Roderick said. "I'll persuade her that she must respect your commands."

"Your skills under the blanket must not be up to your reputation, as ye failed to persuade her yet," Alexander said. "But perhaps she'll find ye more appealing after she spends some time in the dungeon."

Roderick staggered back a step. "You've locked Lily in the dungeon?"

CHAPTER 13

The dungeon was so dark that Lily could not see the rats, but she heard them skittering before her feet as she paced her tiny cell. Rodents were less likely to bite if you kept moving. She had learned that useful lesson when her grown idiot brothers locked her in the cellar, hoping to make her cry and scream, the last time she was fool enough to visit them.

At each turn, she cursed someone. First she cursed the Spaniard for giving her up so easily. As soon as a dozen Highland warriors brandishing huge swords boarded his ship, he pointed to where she was hiding behind a barrel on the deck.

Next she cursed the Lord of the Isles, the great chieftain of chieftains, for sending the men to catch her, and she cursed both him and the men for locking her in this filthy cell.

Then it was Roderick's turn, and that was a long list. She must have walked half a mile back and forth, back and forth, as she cursed him for each wrong he'd done her.

Lastly, she cursed herself for wishing Roderick had been there when the men caught her. Somehow, she did not think she would have ended up in the dungeon if he had been. Like a fool, she had even called for him when they carried her into the cell, though he was nowhere in sight.

She came to an abrupt halt as something else occurred to her. *Good God,* what had she done? Or rather, failed to do.

Now was just a fine time to realize she had never prepared that tincture to prevent conceiving a child from her night of sin with Roderick. How could she have forgotten? Even if she were not locked in this godforsaken dungeon without her bag of herbs, it was far too late now.

She started pacing again, but faster, spinning around again and again in the cramped space. But she could not outrun her thoughts. The reason she had not taken the tincture was painfully clear to her now. Deep down, she wanted a child.

She wanted *his* child.

A door creaked somewhere above her. When she heard footsteps on the stairs that led down to her cell, she finally stopped her pacing.

She squinted against the sudden torchlight that shone through the iron grate of her cell.

"Lily?"

Relief flooded through her at the sound of Roderick's voice, and she chastised herself for it. He had fooled her with false kindness.

She had not let anyone hurt her in a long, long time. No matter what, she would not let the Highlander past her defenses again.

***

Roderick's heart lurched when he saw Lily in the torchlight through the iron grate. She looked much like when he first met her—tired and dirty and dressed in lad's clothes—and utterly pathetic. Thinking she would be more amenable to what he had to say while behind bars, he resisted the urge to unlock the door at once and pull her into his arms.

He leaned against the grate and folded his arms. "I've made a deal with my chieftain to get ye out of there."

"I'm not marrying you," she snapped before he could get out another word. "If that's the agreement you've made, you can tell him I'd rather remain in his dungeon until I rot."

Roderick sighed inwardly. Her brief imprisonment had not cooled her temper.

"I've managed to persuade Alexander to let me take ye to my grandmother's." That had been no easy task after Lily's attempt to defy him by running off. "You'll stay with her for the winter."

"And after the winter?" Lily maintained her defiant stance, but he could tell by the tilt of her head that she was willing to listen now.

"If my grandmother determines ye don't have the gift to be our clan's next seer—"

"I don't."

"Then you'll be free to return to London in the spring with the blessing of the Lord of the Isles."

"You'll understand if I don't have much faith in the old woman's ability to see into the future, as it was her prediction that got me into this trouble," she said. "What if she still says I am the one she foretold?"

"She won't."

"But if she does?" Lily persisted.

"Then you'll have to wed me," he said, "or return to this dungeon until ye rot."

"And what happens to you if I choose the dungeon?" she asked, narrowing her eyes at him.

"I'll be rotting beside ye."

He did not add that Alexander had said he'd throw them into the same cell and leave them there until Lily gave into Roderick's charms—or tired of the rats—and agreed to the marriage.

It never paid to defy the Lord of the Isles.

***

"There's a hot bath waiting for ye in the guest chamber," he said as he unlocked the iron door. "We set sail for Skye in an hour."

Though Lily would be glad to wash off the filth of the dungeon in a hot bath, it annoyed her that Roderick had been so sure she would agree to go to Skye. She only had because it would be far easier to escape from an old woman's cottage than from the Lord of the Isles' dungeon.

"Alexander granted me this time alone with ye," Roderick said, "but there are guards at the top of the stairs who will take ye to your chamber and then to the boat."

"Fine." She started to march past him, but he caught her wrist.

His touch threatened to undermine her control.

"Ye gave me a bad fright when I thought ye were on that ship," he said. "My parents were lost at sea in a winter storm."

"Don't pretend you care," she said, glaring up at him.

"And what were ye thinking, going off on your own at night with drunken warriors everywhere?" he continued. "Then ye put yourself in the hands of that slippery Spaniard when ye must have known he had plans to seduce ye."

"Now that's calling the kettle black," she said. "At least the Spaniard did not plan to trap me forever through deceit."

"I know you're angry," he said, and wiped a smudge from her cheek with his thumb. "But ye can't truly believe I took ye to bed to acquire a seer."

78

"Your performance was impressive," she said. "Your chieftain can't fault you for failing to apply yourself to the task."

A dangerous glint flashed in his eyes. *Good.* She wanted to make him angry.

"Ye think that's all it was?" he bit out.

"*Ach,*" she said, imitating him, "no sacrifice is too great for the clan."

"Damn it, Lily," he said, digging his fingers into her arms. "It wasn't like that, and ye know it."

"It must be a grave disappointment to find out that I'm not who ye thought I was," she said. "All that trouble, and the poor girl doesn't have *The Sight* after all."

Her voice wobbled as she said the last part, which infuriated her.

"Ye could never disappoint me," he said, his eyes fierce. "I don't care if ye have *The Sight.*"

"Since I don't," she said, "will you use your skills in bed to lure another woman here to serve your clan?"

"You're the one I want, the only one," he said through clenched teeth. "For God's sake, Lily, I love ye."

His words sucked the breath out of her. He looked as shocked by what he had said as she was. Even he knew he had gone too far this time.

Her heart could not take any more. She backed away from him until her heel hit the bottom step of the stairs.

"How could you say that?" she said, shaking her head. "You've no cause to hurt me further."

"I should not have said it, not now," he said. "But it is the truth."

"Everything you ever said to me was a lie." She could not fight the tears now, and she wanted to wound him for that final lie. "You've hurt me more than the foul man who raped me in my shop."

He recoiled as if she had slapped him. The pain and shock in his eyes told her she had hit her mark.

"I trusted you!" she shouted, and then she turned and ran up the stairs.

CHAPTER 14

Roderick was in command of the twenty men on the boat, but unlike the last time they sailed, he spoke little to them. He seemed weighed down by sadness—or perhaps it was guilt. He did not speak to Lily at all, except to ask if she needed anything, but his gaze was often on her.

Lily felt herself softening toward him by the hour. He was unfailingly considerate, even tucking wool blankets around her that had been treated with grease to shed the rain. Though he deserved to suffer for deceiving her, Roderick had saved her life and protected her from Harold and the other Douglas men.

When he sat down beside her after two days at sea, she was near to forgiving him. She would not, however, let herself forget that he had tried to control and use her—and he would do it again if she let him.

"This is Skye," he said, nodding toward the island they were fast approaching.

The entire journey through the isles had been breathtaking, but this island, with its rocky shores, green hills dotted with sheep, and blue-gray mountains, was even more beautiful than the rest.

"There's something I need to say to ye before we arrive," he said.

Lily folded her arms and waited for his apology—not that it would make any difference.

"I'm so verra sorry about what happened to ye back in London." His eyes looked haunted as he spoke. "I wish I could kill the man who stole your innocence."

This was not what she had expected him to say.

"I shouldn't have mentioned you in the same breath as that man." She felt a bit guilty herself about throwing that in his face, as if what he had done to her was worse. Though Roderick had hurt her more deeply, that was only because she had allowed herself to trust him.

"I wish ye had told me about it earlier," he said, staring at the sea. "I wouldn't have pressed ye that night if I'd known."

"You didn't have to press me much," she admitted, remembering how she had melted at his first touch. "I wanted to do it."

She waited for the rest of his apology, but he seemed to have nothing else to say to her.

"Is that all you feel guilty for?" she finally asked him. "Not for deceiving me and trying to trap me here for the rest of my life?"

"I never meant to force ye to stay past the winter storms." He shrugged. "I thought if ye were meant to be our seer, ye would come to see that yourself. If not, you'd go."

"Don't lie to me again," she said between clenched teeth. "Your grandmother told you I was the next seer, and you believed her."

"Truly, I could not be sure what my grandmother meant to tell me," he said. "Once ye meet her, ye might understand."

If he were not twice her size, she would throw him overboard. Instead, she turned away from him and fixed her gaze on the shoreline of the island.

They were both silent as the boat rounded a point and sailed into a large inlet bordered by green rolling hills on one side and rocky cliffs and mountains on the other. Her curiosity got the better of her when the men sailed the boat to the mountainous side and into a small, deserted bay next to a sheer rock cliff.

"Why are we stopping here?" she asked. "Is there something wrong with the boat?"

"My grandmother's cottage is here," Roderick said, pointing straight up.

Lily tilted her head back. Now she understood why Roderick and the Lord of the Isles were not concerned she would run away from the old woman's cottage.

"There's not even a village," she said, looking at the empty beach.

"I fear it will be quite dull, especially for a London lass," he said after he lifted her down from the boat. "But 'tis better than spending the winter in a cold dungeon."

That did not sound encouraging. As escape appeared unlikely, she tried to adjust to the notion of being in this desolate place for the entire winter.

"I'll be across the inlet at Dunscaith Castle," he said, pointing to the impressive fortress on the opposite shore. "I'll sail over every week or so to see how the two of ye fare."

"You're leaving me alone here?"

"I must return to my duties," he said. "I'm captain of the guard at the castle."

He led her to where rough-hewn steps had been cut into the side of the cliff.

"The steps to the cottage are slippery when it's wet, which is most the time in the winter, so be careful," Roderick said. "Go first so I can catch ye if ye fall."

Good heavens, he was not joking. She imagined herself plunging into the sea, but she was not about to let him know that she was frightened half to death. After saying a prayer, she started up. The climb up the side of the cliff was harrowing and so steep that she was soon out of breath.

"Anything else ye ought to warn me about?" she said between gasps for air when they were finally nearing the top.

Roderick emitted what sounded like a string of curses in Gaelic. "I've told her time and again not to do that. One day, she'll fall into the sea."

Lily followed his gaze upward and gasped when she saw a figure with gray hair and a wizened face leaning precariously over the edge to peer down at them. The woman must be mad.

"There is one more thing I should warn ye about," he said as they continued up. "My grandmother speaks only Gaelic."

So, Lily could not even speak with the mad old woman she would be alone with for weeks on end. Perhaps she should have stayed in the dungeon.

"But it won't matter much," he added, "as she usually knows what you're thinking."

***

The moment Lily entered the cottage and saw the rows of drying herbs hanging from the rafters and the shelves filled with bottles and vials, her face lit up like she'd come home.

"Oh!" she said, clasping her hands together. "This is so much like my shop."

Roderick had not seen Lily smile since the bonfire, and it did his heart good.

"I don't recognize that plant," she said, crossing the tiny cottage to examine a bunch of tied herbs hanging next to the hearth.

Before he could introduce them, she and his grandmother were chattering, each in her own language, as Lily pointed to various herbs or picked up vials and sniffed them. After a time, his grandmother waved Lily onto a stool and set a hot drink next to her on the table. Her feisty terrier made his appearance then. Lily's laughter filled the cottage when the wee dog jumped into her lap and started licking her face.

Roderick told himself he could leave with peace of mind now, knowing she would not be so miserable here after all.

But there would be no peace for him.

His grandmother met his gaze, and he knew she saw into his heart. With Lily diverted, she sidled over to him.

"She's not our next seer, is she?" he asked.

"Nay, she's not."

"That means she'll leave," he said, his heart sinking to his feet. "What am I to do, Seanmhair?"

"Ye must persuade her to stay." She patted his arm and recited the old expression, *"Chan ann leis a'chiad bhuille thuiteas a'chraobh." 'Tis not with the first stroke that the tree falls.*

***

Lily hummed to herself as she and Seanmhair hung greenery over the door. The smells of the delicious venison stew they had made earlier filled the cottage. Odd, how this was so much like her mad ramblings about that healer who lived on the border before Roderick found her.

Seanmhair gave her a smug smile and pointed to herself. Apparently, the old woman believed she had put that dream in Lily's head and it was her in it. Seanmhair practiced ancient magic, so perhaps she had done it.

"'Tis lucky ye live here," Lily told her. "If people in London saw you tossing herbs on the fire and mumbling chants, they'd burn you, for certain."

She sighed when Seanmhair spoke what Lily assumed were the same words in Gaelic and motioned impatiently for Lily to repeat them. The woman did this to her all day long.

"I'll be leaving in a few weeks," Lily reminded her, as she did every day, then she repeated it in Gaelic without prompting since she knew the words well by now.

Seanmhair rocked from side to side as she mumbled another chant. The old woman was strange, but she was good company, and Lily had grown fond of her in the week since her arrival.

"Will you teach me some of those spells?" Lily asked with a laugh.

She understood enough of Seanmhair's reply to gather that the answer was an emphatic no, but Lily intended to wheedle a few spells out of her eventually.

"Roderick," the old woman said, with a nod toward the door.

Lily's pulse jumped. She swiped uselessly at her ungovernable hair and brushed her palms on the skirt of her gown. Though he came nearly every day, she always felt unprepared to see him.

The door opened with a rush of cold air, and Roderick filled the doorway looking so handsome she had to stifle a sigh.

Seanmhair poked Lily's shoulder and handed her the cloak she had stolen from the baker's son a lifetime ago.

"All right, we're going." Lily spoke the simple words in Gaelic without thinking.

As if to reward her, Seanmhair broke off a piece of greenery from the pile on the table that they had gathered earlier and stuck it in Lily's hair.

"Thank you," Lily said in Gaelic.

Roderick winked at his grandmother and took Lily's arm. Lily was well aware that the two were working together to persuade her not to return to London in the spring. She did not quite know what to make of it, for surely his grandmother at least knew Lily did not have the makings of a great seer.

Lily and Roderick walked the path along the cliff, as they usually did. Each time he came to the cottage, she felt her defenses weaken.

"Aren't you needed at the castle?"

"We've no enemies likely to attack while Alexander is at peace with the Crown, and we've plenty of well-trained warriors at the castle." He paused. "What we will need soon is a healer, as my grandmother fears she'll no longer be able to make the trip across the inlet come spring."

The sail across the inlet was short, and the old woman seemed well enough to Lily.

As they walked side by side, she felt his desire as if it were something physical pulling their bodies together. To break the spell, she stepped off the path. The view from the cliff usually soothed her.

"'Tis so beautiful here," she said, as she took in the wide vista of the sea dotted with islands and the dreamlike layers of gray-blue mountains on the mainland beyond.

"I didn't expect ye to like Skye," he said as he came to stand beside her. "I feared you'd suffer from loneliness in such a quiet place."

Lily liked the quiet, and she was accustomed to keeping her own company. At least here, she had his grandmother and Roderick's visits. In truth, she had not realized how lonely her life in London had become since her sister married and the old healer died. She was not about to confess that, however.

"Anyone would appreciate how lovely it is here," she said.

"Maigrid hated it," Roderick said, staring at the horizon.

"I can tell that her leaving still pains you."

"She hurt my pride, that's all." He shrugged. "We weren't suited. Ach, she even hated my grandmother."

"Hated Seanmhair?" Lily was appalled. "I regret not slapping that woman when I had the chance."

"Seanmhair feels much the same," he said. "I had to talk her out of casting a spell to cover Maigrid in boils."

Lily was laughing when Roderick turned her to face him and plucked the sprig from her hair. When she saw that it was mistletoe, she swallowed hard. She liked his grandmother, but the old woman was a sly dog.

"Seanmhair says 'tis verra, verra bad luck to refuse a kiss under mistletoe," he said with a devilish grin. "And she knows such things."

Lily told herself that a brief, lighthearted kiss would be harmless, but she knew it was a lie. She was playing with fire—and she didn't care.

As he leaned toward her, her heart raced and she rose up on her toes. His lips barely brushed hers at first, and yet the kiss set off a burst of longing like the torch that exploded the bonfire into flame at the Yuletide celebration.

She held on to Roderick as if her life depended upon it as they devoured each other with hot, hungry kisses. When he backed her against the lone tree on the cliff and lifted her off her feet, she wrapped her legs around him.

Waves crashed below them, the surf echoing the storm of passion between them. *Yes. Yes. Yes.* His hands seemed to be everywhere at once, massaging her breasts, running along her thighs, squeezing her backside. She had missed him so much.

Roderick got control of himself first and leaned back, panting. Why did he stop? She could feel his hard shaft against her through their clothes. Oh, how she wanted him.

"My grandmother knew the moment she saw ye that you're not the next seer," he said. "You'll be free to go, if ye still want to."

Lily still felt dazed with passion and struggled to understand why he was speaking of this now.

"But ye don't have to leave," he said, his dark blue eyes searching her face. "Ye can change your mind and stay."

"I have my shop and..." She could not think of a single other reason for returning. After a long moment, she asked, "Why should I stay?"

"Because I love ye," he said. "I want ye to be my wife."

As she looked into Roderick's beautiful face, he appeared so sincere. Dare she believe him? No one had ever loved her, except her sister and Linnet.

"Ye belong here," he said. "Ye belong with me."

She was so confused that she did not know what she wanted or what was true anymore.

"But if you're going to leave," he said, cupping her face, "I don't want to do this."

She realized she still had her back against the tree and her legs were wrapped around his hips. He was right—this was not something she ought to decide in the midst of passion. Until now,

86

she had not seriously contemplated remaining here, marrying Roderick—or marrying at all. She needed time to think. She dropped her legs, and he set her on her feet.

"We should go back," she said, and started off without him.

CHAPTER 15

Roderick had not visited the cottage in three days.

Lily found herself looking toward the door again and again. Had he given up on her? She was glad that Seanmhair kept her busy, cleaning her cottage from top to bottom for the new year, or Hogmanay, but the old woman was in a foul mood.

Lily had become quite good at deciphering the instructions Seanmhair gave her in a mix of Gaelic and gestures. Yet Seanmhair was impatient as she handed her the broom and indicated that Lily must sweep the ashes from the hearth to sweep out the bad luck of the past year and start the new year fresh. After Lily carried the ashes outside, Seanmhair motioned for her to take a long walk and not come back soon.

Lily took Seanmhair's little dog Beag with her to keep her company. As she watched him race after a squirrel, she thought a dog like Beag would be good at keeping the rats out of her shop. But would he be happy in the city, crowded with people and buildings?

Would she be happy?

She had told herself that she never wanted a husband, a man who would try to control her and steal her earnings. Yet the notion of being married to Roderick did not strike her in the same way. Though he could be heavy-handed when he believed her safety was at risk, he would not interfere with her work as a healer. He certainly respected his grandmother, and he'd made it clear he would be pleased to have Lily serve as the castle's healer.

She had been content in London, but that was before she had come to this island. As she continued her walk, she drank in the beauty of the mountains and sea, the fresh scents in the clean air, and the freedom of scrambling over the rocky hillside. She would miss all of these pleasures, but she could survive without them.

She was less certain she could survive without Roderick.

And she did not want to.

"Come," she called to the dog as she turned around. "If he'll still have me, I'm going to stay."

***

"Where's Lily?" Roderick asked as he entered the cottage.

"I sent her out with Beag," Seanmhair said, with an impatient wave of her hand. "The lass is learning our language so quickly that we cannot say what we must with her here."

"I don't know what else I can do." Roderick paced the tiny cottage feeling like a caged animal. "She doesn't want to be my wife."

"Ye must keep her here."

"I could use your help, Seanmhair," he said. "Give me one of your potions."

"There are potions for lust," she said, shaking her head. "But love is a magic all its own and must find its own way."

"Lust is a good start," he said. "Give me the potion for that."

"The two of ye have no need for that," she said, rolling her eyes.

Most women wanted a man to protect them and give them a home. But Lily had made it plain from the start that she neither needed nor wanted a husband. He understood she was a skittish lass, like a wild horse who shied at the sight of a bridle. He wanted to take care of her, not trap her. He must find a reason for her to marry him.

What does Lily want? What can I give her?

"All of this," his grandmother said, spreading her arms. "She wants a true home with a clan and a family—though she's too stubborn to admit it. Most of all, she wants you, Roderick."

Lily wanted him in her bed—but not for long and not as a husband.

"She's one of those lost souls who had the misfortune of being born at the wrong place and into the wrong family," Seanmhair said. "The mistrust they taught her is a grave challenge."

His grandmother was being no help at all.

"But ye must keep the lass here," his grandmother said. "She is the answer."

"Don't try to tell me again that she's the clan's next seer." He dropped onto a stool and ran his hands through his hair. "How could ye have it so wrong? Lily doesn't have the damned *Sight* at all, let alone the gift of a great seer."

"Lily does have a touch of the gift, like most good healers," she said. "'Tis just as I expected."

"As ye expected?" he said, looking up. "Then why did ye plant the notion of her being our next seer in my head in the first place?"

"I never said ye would find the seer on your journey."

"Ye did," he said.

She sat down beside him and patted his shoulder. "What I said was that ye would find the lass *you* need, Roderick. Lily is meant to be your wife."

That was not how he remembered it, but she was right that Lily was the lass he needed.

"Why did ye not tell me all this from the start?" he said. "I would have done things differently if I'd known Lily was meant to be my wife."

"Hmmph," his grandmother snorted. "If you'd known it, ye would have made things even worse than ye have."

It was true that he had been desperate to avoid marriage.

"Though Lily is no' much of a seer," his grandmother said, "she is also the lass the clan needs."

"To hell with what the clan needs," he muttered, and rubbed his hands over his face.

"*The Sight* was verra strong in your mother," she said. "Ye carry her blood."

If his grandmother could not tell him something useful, he wished she would be quiet so he could think.

"The gift rarely shows itself in the men of our family," she continued. "But it comes out in you when Lily needs ye most. 'Tis why ye found her on that hillside."

Ach, what was she droning on about? He didn't have *The Sight*.

"The child born of your blood and a true love will have a powerful gift that surpasses even mine," she said. "'Tis not Lily, but the daughter the two of ye will have together, who is destined to become a great seer of our clan."

Roderick had barely been listening to her rambling, but he jolted upright when her words penetrated his thoughts. "What did ye say?"

"I saw it in a vision as clear as the nose on my face," she said, laying her finger against the side of her nose. "Your daughter will take my place and serve our clan through difficult times and for many, many years."

"Lily and I will have a child together?" The notion sent a burst of joy through him. "A daughter?"

Roderick imagined a wee girl with red hair as bright as the sun and startling green eyes.

"Aye, and several other bairns as well—if ye don't lose the mother." His grandmother gave him a sharp slap on the back of his head. "The vision is fading, so you'd best win her back."

He kissed his grandmother's cheek and got up to go after Lily. At the door he paused.

"Lily must not know of this," he said. "If I'm to have any chance at all of persuading her to stay and be my wife, she cannot learn of it."

His grandmother raised her hands and shook her head, but he was intent on this. The last thing he needed was for Lily to believe he had any motive for keeping her here other than that he loved her.

"Lily must never learn that your vision was of our child, and not her, becoming the seer."

"'Tis too late," his grandmother said. "The lass already knows. She's listening at the door."

***

Lily felt so light that her feet seemed to barely touch the ground as she raced back to the cottage. Not even the cold drizzle that had started to fall could dampen her spirits. She had decided to trust her heart and marry Roderick.

When she reached the cottage, she heard voices inside, including the deep tones that played on her heartstrings.

Old habits die hard. Listening at doors had helped her avoid getting caught in her family's criminal schemes and other dangers in the city. Before she realized what she was doing, she paused to listen.

"Lily must not know of this..."

Lily sucked in her breath. What was Roderick keeping from her? She tried to persuade herself that she had misunderstood as she pressed her ear against the door. Though she did not understand all the words, the few she did were damning.

"... stay...be my wife... she cannot learn..."

Roderick had deceived her again. He'd told her it was love, but he had another reason for keeping her here. There was something he wanted from her. She held her breath, desperate to hear what it was.

"… *your vision was of our child… the seer.*"

Tears blurred Lily's eyes as she ran from the cottage. She heard the door slam but kept running until Roderick caught her.

"I hate you! I hate you!" she shouted as she scratched and kicked at him. "How could you do this to me!"

"I know what ye overheard sounded bad," he said, holding her arms. "But ye must give me a chance to explain."

"You pretended that you loved me," she said. "But you only want me for the child you think I can give to your clan. That's all it ever was."

"Children would be a blessing," he said. "But I want to marry ye because I can't live without ye. Lily, I love ye with all my heart."

"I'll never be your wife," she shouted. "I won't stay here! I'm going back to my shop in London."

"Ye want to throw away the happiness we could have," he said, sounding angry now. "And for what? For four walls and some hanging herbs?"

"I have customers who rely on me, people I help."

"They pay coin for your service, but will they help you when you're in trouble? Nay, they care nothing for ye," he said. "'Tis not like serving your own people, your clan, who are bonded to ye in good times and bad."

She remembered how she had felt embraced in the joy of his clan at the Yuletide bonfire—and how alone she usually felt on feast days. Yet the sense of kinship with his clan that marriage would bring could never outweigh the pain of loving a man who used and deceived her.

And she did love Roderick.

"Look into your heart, Lily," Roderick said, bringing his face close to hers. "Ye belong here. Ye belong with me."

"I don't care," she said, shaking her head. "I won't stay."

He gripped her arms and held her so that their bodies almost touched, which caused a yearning that nearly undid her.

"When you're back in your London town," he said, "you'll miss the sound of the sea outside the window, the mist on the loch, the mountains shrouded in clouds."

As he spoke, each image was clear to her mind.

"And you'll miss me." His voice was thick with emotion, and his eyes locked on hers. "You'll sit alone by your hearth on a cold evening with no one to hear the stories of your day—a strange malady ye treated or a new cure ye tried—and you'll wish I was there."

It was true, all of it. But it changed nothing.

"And at night," he said, "you'll lie alone in your bed thinking of the pleasure I could give ye."

She would long for his touch and miss him every night and day. But she would not give him the satisfaction of admitting it.

"Who's to say I'll be alone in my bed?" she snapped.

The sudden rage burning in his eyes tested her courage. She swallowed hard and stood her ground. Though he was a lying bastard who broke her heart, she knew he would not harm her physically.

"'Tis nothing to me what ye do when ye leave here," he said, but the twitch in his eye told her he lied. "Ye can be sure I won't be sleeping alone."

His words felt like a blow to her chest, forcing the air out of her lungs.

"I expect I'll be wed," he said, "and have a babe on the way by spring."

Her eyes stung. That babe could be hers. Should be hers.

"Will ye lie to her as well?" she asked. "Tell her that ye love her?"

"I wish I could tell her that because a good woman deserves her man's love," he said. "Though I can't give her love, I'll do my damnedest to be the best husband to her that I can."

With that, he turned his back on her. Lily let the tears slide down her face as she watched him walk away with long, purposeful strides.

***

When Lily opened the door, she found Seanmhair bustling about the cottage, gathering things into a leather bag. The old woman paused to give Lily a scathing look.

Lily was already in a state. She hoped she would not lose the old woman's friendship over her refusal to wed Roderick.

"Stubborn as an ass," Seanmhair mumbled loud enough for Lily to hear. "A shame there's no cure for that."

Lily was taken aback by Seanmhair's hurtful words. Though she only understood half of what the old woman spewed, that was more than enough.

"Selfish...inconsiderate...dimwitted...."

Lily went to stand before the old woman. "I'm not those things."

"Hmmph." Seanmhair conveyed as much disgust in that Scottish snort as Roderick did. She made a swiping motion with her hand as she said, "Ye tossed away the love of a good man."

"He doesn't truly care for me," Lily said, clenching her fists. "It was all lies."

"Any fool could see," Seanmhair said, leaning forward and tapping her finger next to her eye, "my grandson is lovesick for ye."

"Where are you going?" Lily asked when Seanmhair wrapped a plaid around her shoulders and opened the door. "It will be dark soon."

"With Roderick," Seanmhair said, and whistled to her dog.

"You're taking Beag too?" Lily asked as the dog trotted out.

After Seanmhair slammed the door, Lily sat down hard on the closest stool. Roderick's and the old woman's words spun inside her head.

Ye tossed away the love of a good man... And for what? For four walls and some hanging herbs...I'll be wed with a babe on the way by spring...

She must have sat there, stunned, for a long time because the cottage was now pitch black. She fumbled for the lamp on the table and lit it. Waves of grief struck her as she looked around the cottage. She had been happy during her short time here.

In her mind's eye, she saw Roderick ducking his head under the low doorframe and sharing a laugh with his grandmother. He was so good to the old woman. With a sharp pain of longing, it struck her that he would make a good and kind father as well.

Unable to bear being alone in the cottage another moment, she grabbed her cloak. As she started to leave, she noticed the candle Seanmhair had set in the window, intending to light it for the

94

Hogmanay night, and she felt compelled to respect the old woman's wishes. Though Lily would not go far, the candle would help her find the cottage in the darkness.

The path along the cliff was in deep mud from the ceaseless rain. Slipping and sliding, she found herself running down it as if she could outrun her thoughts. When she finally stopped, she stood gasping for air and holding her side as she stared out at the whitecaps that covered the black sea. The crash of the waves far below sounded like a rebuke, telling her she was a fool, again and again.

Lily squeezed her eyes closed, trying to shut out the pain. God help her, what had she done? Seanmhair's voice filled her head. *Ye tossed away the love of a good man.*

Suddenly the ground beneath her gave way, and she was falling into the black night.

CHAPTER 16

"Roderick!" Lily called his name as she flung her arms and legs out, desperate to stop her slide toward the edge of the cliff.

When something slammed into her side, she grabbed hold of it. She held on, hugging it to her chest, as rocks and dirt hit her, threatening to take her over the side. When everything stopped moving, her feet were dangling in the air. She spit the dirt out of her mouth, but she could not wipe the dirt from her eyes without letting go. Through the grit, she saw that what had saved her was a stubborn, stunted tree that grew out of the side of the rock face several feet below where the path had been.

The tree trunk she was clinging to was only four or five inches wide. If she could stand on it, she might be able to reach the top of the cliff. She tried to swing her legs up onto it, and gasped when the tree creaked and tilted farther out over the gaping emptiness below her. Her heart beat frantically. How long could she hold on?

Roderick, come find me. She knew he was at the castle and could not hear her, and yet she called his name over and over in her head.

As she hung there, bruised and bleeding and facing certain death, everything became clear to her. The men of her family were feckless. They had taught her the hard lesson that she could not rely on anyone but herself. But Roderick was nothing like them. If he knew she was here, he would save her. He would not hesitate to put her life before his.

The icy rain numbed her fingers, making it increasingly difficult to hold on. But she remembered how Roderick had somehow found her when she was near death on that hillside, and she began to hope.

As the long minutes passed, she thought about how she had prided herself on her strength, and yet had let fear rule her—fear that she would be used, disappointed, pathetic, and heartbroken. Despite what she had overheard outside the cottage, her heart told her that

Roderick was worthy of her faith. Finding such a man was an unexpected gift.

A gift she had refused.

And yet she was certain now that he would come for her. Her arms ached from holding herself up, and she had begun to shake violently from the penetrating cold.

She did not have much time left.

***

With a heavy heart, Roderick climbed the treacherous steps cut into the side of the cliff in the dark and pouring rain, one more foolish act. He did not know what made him decide to sail back across the inlet as soon as he'd set his grandmother on the shore by the castle, but something compelled him to return. How many times did Lily need to tell him nay before he gave up?

It was after midnight, but she had left a candle in the window, a tiny beacon of light giving him hope on this dismal night. He hesitated outside the door. What more could he say to persuade her? He was out of words.

Apprehension, sudden and urgent, swept over him like a crashing wave. Without knocking, he flung the door open. One glance told him the cottage was empty. The candle had not burned down much, so Lily could not have been gone long.

Where was she? She was in trouble, he knew it.

Roderick.

He heard her voice in his head, pulling him as if a twine connected their hearts. He quickly found his grandmother's old lantern and a rope and ran back outside. Icy rain pelted his face as he held the lantern high, trying to see into the blackness. On the sharp wind, he heard her call his name again. He had to find her.

Lily, where are ye?

Roderick had never had a vision in his life, but now he saw Lily with her arms wrapped around a small tree as clearly as if she were right in front of him. He sensed her growing weakness, and her deep cold was so real to him that a shiver went up his back. He must find her quickly.

He pushed back his rising panic and searched his memory. As a lad, he had scrambled all over this part of the island, and he knew every inch of the path along the cliff. He must recognize something from his vision that would tell him where she was. In his mind's eye, he followed the path along the cliff. He remembered seeing a tree bent by the wind and growing sideways out of the rock with its roots clinging to the side of the cliff. That was it.

He knew exactly where she was, and it was not far. He took off at a run down the muddy path, which was quickly turning to ice with the increasing cold.

When he neared the part of the cliff where the tree was, he saw that the path had been washed out.

"Lily! Lily!" he called out as he leaned over the side of the cliff, holding the lantern out.

Amidst the browns and grays of the rocks, the lantern picked up the glint of Lily's red hair. *Jesu.* His heart went to his throat when he saw the white surf of the waves crashing two hundred feet below her dangling feet.

"Hold on!" he shouted. "Hold on!"

He set the lantern on the ground close to the edge where it would shed some light on the side of the cliff. As Lily was bound to be too weak to hold a rope, he would have to go down for her. So near the slide, the ground would be unstable. It would be easy to set off another slide, so he would have to be careful and avoid the weakest area as much as he could.

After tying one end of the rope around a boulder and the other around his waist, he started down. He rappelled down the cliff until he was on a level with her, then inched sideways.

"Lily, stay awake!" he shouted when he saw that she had rested her head on the tree trunk.

She did not respond, and he feared she would lose her grip and fall before he could reach her. When he could almost touch her, she lifted her head.

"I can't hold any longer," she whispered.

As she started to fall, he dove to the side and caught her around the waist with one arm. But he'd thrown himself off balance and banged against the side of the cliff. He quickly found his footing again, but he'd started a small slide. Fearing it would grow, he raced up the rope, protecting Lily from the flying rocks and debris as best he could.

When he made it to the top, he untied the rope and ran with Lily in his arms until they were a safe distance from the slide. He heard a crack and a thunderous crash and turned in time to see an entire stretch of the cliff break off and fall into the sea.

He fell to his knees and held Lily tightly in his arms.

Praise God, he had found her in time.

"I knew you'd come," she said, and wrapped her arms around his neck.

"I always will," he said.

"I know that now," she said.

When he got her back to the cottage, he bundled her in blankets, gave her a cup of hot whisky, and sat her on his lap before the hearth. His heart might never recover from this night, but Lily seemed to revive quickly.

Once she did, she took him to bed and tested the strength of his heart again. And in the morning, she insisted they go back to where he had rescued her the night before.

The cliff looked like a cleaver had shorn it, and there was a huge a pile of rocks on the shore below it.

Lily turned to him and held out her hand. In her palm lay the key to her shop, the one she had been so frantic to find after they had made love the first time.

She closed her hand around the key and then flung it off the cliff.

"I take it that means you're staying?" he asked, a smile tugging at the corners of his mouth.

"My home is where you are," she said. "Always and forever."

Then she threw her arms around him and gave him a kiss to remember.

EPILOGUE

"Da is here!"

Lily turned from where she was hanging boughs over the cottage door to look at her six-year-old daughter. "Are ye certain, Teàrlag?"

Roderick had said not to expect him until much later.

"Aye," her daughter said. "My brothers too."

At times Lily found it unnerving how strong *The Sight* was in her small daughter.

"They brought a present for me," Teàrlag said.

"It's meant to be a surprise," Lily reprimanded her. "Ye know ye shouldn't look."

Her daughter lifted her shoulders and gave her an unrepentant grin.

They had lost Seanmhair earlier this year, and Lily had wanted to return to the cottage to clean and decorate it for the Yuletide as Roderick's grandmother would have done. In the morning, they would all return to the castle.

"Da and my brothers are verra hungry," Teàrlag said, tugging at her skirts.

Lily just had time to set the bowls for the venison stew on the table when her three sons burst into the cottage with a cold wind and boisterous greetings. They smelled of damp wool, dogs, and fresh pine boughs. They were strapping lads who would become fine men and great warriors, a credit to their clan like their father. She was so proud of them.

Roderick entered last, ducking his head through the doorway. The sight of him still made her heart flutter.

Later that night after the children were asleep in the loft, Lily lay in her husband's arms, watching the flickering flames in the hearth and thinking about how lucky she was.

"Do you think we would have found each other," she asked, "if your grandmother had not had that vision and persuaded the Lord of the Isles to send you into the Lowlands?"

"Aye," he said. "We were meant to be together."

"That we were," she said, smiling up at him.

"She told me that love has a magic all its own." He kissed her forehead. "One way or another, I would have found ye."

THE END

AUTHOR'S NOTE

This novella is not part of a series, but I had fun giving it small ties to all three of my historical romance series. Fans of my THE RETURN OF THE HIGHLANDERS series have been asking for more stories about handsome MacDonald warriors from the Isle of Skye, so Roderick is for them. I made him the father of a secondary character in that series, which also makes him distantly related to three of the four heroes. Lily, my heroine here, was a child character in *Knight of Passion*, the final book in my ALL THE KING'S MEN trilogy.

Finally, the Douglas chieftain mentioned in this story was the 3rd Earl of Angus, a predecessor of Archibald Douglas, the 6th Earl of Angus, whose ambitions cause such trouble for his sisters in my latest series, THE DOUGLAS LEGACY. The Douglas earls and the Lord of the Isles were real historical figures. As always, I like to advise readers that fact and legend blur after hundreds of years and that, as a fiction writer, I take as much latitude as I need to write a good story.

An Excerpt from **CAPTURED BY A LAIRD**, book 1 in
Margaret Mallory's new series, **The Douglas Legacy**

Scotland
1517

Burning her husband's bed was a mistake. Alison could see that
now.

Yet each time she passed the rectangle of charred earth as she
paced the castle courtyard, she felt a wave of satisfaction. She had
waited to commit her act of rebellion until her daughters were
asleep. But that night, after her husband's body was taken to the
priory for burial, she ordered the servants to carry the bed out of the
keep. She set fire to it herself. The castle household, accustomed to
the meek mistress her husband had required her to be, was
thoroughly shocked.

"Do ye see them yet?" Alison called up to one of the guards on
the wall.

When the guard shook his head, she resumed her pacing. Where
were her brothers? They had sent word this morning that they were
on their way.

As she passed the scorched patch again, she recalled how the
flames shot up into the night sky. She had stood watching the fire
until dawn, imagining the ugliness of the past years turning to black
ashes like the bed. The memories did not burn away, but she did feel
cleaner.

Destroying such an expensive piece of furniture was self-
indulgent, but that was not why she counted burning it a mistake.
While she could not tolerate having that bed in her home, it would
have been wiser to give it away or sell it. And yet she simply could
not in good conscience pass it on to someone else. Not when she felt
as if the bed itself carried an evil.

Instinctively, she touched the black quartz pendant at her throat
that her mother had given her to ward off ill luck. It had been
missing since Blackadder broke the chain on their wedding night.
After the fire, she found it wedged in a crack in the floor where the
bed had been.

"Lady Alison!" a guard shouted down from the wall. "They're

here!"

The heavy wooden gates swung open, and her two brothers galloped over the drawbridge followed by scores of Douglas warriors. *Praise God*. As the castle filled with her clansmen, Alison immediately felt safer.

One look at Archie's thunderous expression, however, told her that his meeting with the queen had not gone well. Without a word, her brothers climbed the steps of the keep, crossed the hall where platters of food were being set out on the long trestle tables for the Douglas warriors, and continued up the stairs to the private chambers. They never discussed family business in front of others.

"She is my wife!" Archie said as soon they were behind closed doors. "How dare she think she can dismiss me as if I were one of her servants?"

Alison tapped her foot, trying to be patient, while her brother, the 6th Earl of Angus and chieftain of the Douglas clan, stormed up and down the length of the room. When Archie's back was to her, she exchanged a look with George, her more clever brother, and rolled her eyes. This was all so predictable.

"I warned ye not to be so blatant about your affair with Lady Jane," George said in a mild tone.

"My affairs are none of my wife's concern," Archie snapped.

"A queen is not an ordinary wife," George said as he poured himself and Archie cups of wine from the side table.

Alison found it ironic that the Douglas clan owed the greatest rise in their fortunes to Archie's liaison with the widowed queen. Usually, it was the ladies of the family who were tasked with securing royal favor via the bedchamber.

Archie, always overconfident, had gone too far. While the Council had been willing to tolerate the queen's foolishness in taking the young Douglas chieftain as her lover, they were livid when the pair wed in secret, making Archie the infant king's stepfather. The Council responded by removing the queen as regent. She fled to England amidst accusations that she had tried to abscond with the royal heir.

"How was I to know my wife would return to Scotland?" Archie said, raising his arms. "Besides, I'm a young man. She couldn't expect me to live like a monk while she was gone."

Doubtless, the queen, who was pregnant with Archie's child

when she fled, expected her husband to join her. But while the queen paid a lengthy visit on her brother Henry VIII, the Douglas men retreated behind the high walls of Tantallon Castle and waited for the cries of treason to subside.

That was two years ago. And now, Albany, the man who replaced the queen as regent, was on a ship back to France, and the queen was returning. Archie had gone to meet her at Berwick Castle, just across the border.

"Is there no hope of reconciling with her?" Alison ventured to ask.

"I bedded that revolting woman four times in two days—and for naught!" Archie thrust his hand out. "I had her in my palm again, I swear it. But then some villain sent her a message informing her about Jane."

"Must have been the Hamiltons," George said, referring to their greatest rivals.

"Despite that setback, I managed to persuade the queen—through great effort, I might add—that we should enter Edinburgh together as man and wife for all the members of the damned Council to see," Archie said, his blue eyes flashing. "But then she discovered I'd been collecting the rents on her dower lands and flew into a rage."

No wonder the queen was angry. After abandoning her, Archie had lived openly with his lover and their newborn daughter in one of the queen's dower castles—and on the queen's money.

"You're her husband," George said, leaning back in his chair. "Ye had every right to collect her rents. Still do."

Alison did not want to hear about husbands and their rights. She folded her arms and tamped down her impatience while she waited for the right moment to ask.

"Enough talk. We must join the men." Archie threw back his cup of wine. "We'll ride for Edinburgh as soon as they've eaten their fill."

George was already on his feet. She could wait no longer.

"Ye must leave some of our Douglas warriors here to protect this castle," she blurted out. "The Blackadder men are deserting me."

She hoped her brothers would not ask why. She did not want to explain that burning her husband's bed had insulted the Blackadder men and spurred many of them to leave. They disliked having a woman in command of the castle, and she had unwittingly given them the excuse they needed.

"I can't spare any men now," Archie said, slapping his gloves against his hand. "I must gather all my forces in a show of strength to convince my pigheaded wife that she needs my help to regain the Regency."

"The Hamiltons will attempt to do the same," George added.

"But what about me and my daughters?" Alison demanded. "What about the Blackadder lands Grandfather thought were so important that I was forced to wed that man? I was a child of thirteen!"

"For God's sake, Alison, we're in a fight for control of the crown," Archie said. "That will not be decided at Blackadder Castle."

"Please, I need your help." She clutched Archie's arm as he started toward the door. "Ye promised to protect us."

Archie came to an abrupt halt, and the shared memory hung between them like a dead rat.

"Mother did not need to remind me of my duty to my family," he said between clenched teeth. "And neither do you."

Unlike the Douglas men, who lauded Archie's seduction of the queen as a boon for the family, their mother begged him to end the affair. A generation ago, one of her sisters had been the king's mistress. After it was rumored that the king had fallen so in love that he wished to marry her, all three of their mother's sisters died mysteriously.

When Archie wed the queen in secret, knowing full well that every other powerful family in Scotland would oppose the marriage, their mother made one demand of her sons. Archie and George promised her, on their father's grave, that they would protect their four sisters.

"I'll find ye a new husband as soon as these other matters are settled," Archie said. "You'll be safe here until then."

Another husband was not what Alison asked for and was the last thing she wanted. "What I need are warriors—"

"Who would dare attack you?" Archie said. "Now that we are rid of Albany, I am the man most likely to rule Scotland."

Before she could argue, Archie pushed past her and disappeared down the circular stone stairwell.

"Don't fret, Allie," George said, and gave her a kiss on her cheek. "Your most dangerous neighbors were the Hume lairds, and they're both dead."

***

David Hume left his horse and warriors a safe distance outside the city walls and proceeded on foot. If the guards were watching for him, they would not expect him to come alone, or so he hoped. Keeping his hood low over his face and his hand on his dirk, he mingled with the men herding cattle through the Cowgate Port to sell in the city's market.

A month ago, David would have been amused to find himself entering the great city of Edinburgh between two cows. But his humor had been wrung from him. As he walked up West Bow toward the center of the city, the rage that was always with him now swelled until his skin felt too tight.

He paused before entering the High Street and scraped the dung off his boots while he scanned the bustling street for anyone who might attempt to thwart him. Then, keeping watch on the armed men amidst the merchants, well-dressed ladies, beggars, and thieves, he started down the hill in the direction of Holyrood Palace. He spared a glance over his shoulder at Edinburgh Castle, the massive fortress that sat atop the black rock behind him. If he were caught, he would likely grow old in its bleak dungeon. He'd prefer a quick death.

David had walked this very street with his father and uncle. With each step, he tried to imagine how that day might have ended differently. Could he have stopped it? Perhaps, perhaps not. Regardless, he should have tried. From the moment they entered Holyrood Palace, he had sensed the danger. It pricked at the back of his neck and made his hands itch to pull his blade.

The Hume lairds had been guaranteed safe conduct. Relying on that pledge of honor made in the king's name, David did not follow his instincts, did not shout to their men to fight their way out. Instead, he watched his father and uncle relinquish their weapons at the palace door, and he did the same.

Never again.

When he saw the stone arches of St. Giles jutting into the High Street, David's heart beat so hard it hurt. The church was next to the Tolbooth, the prison where the royal guards brought his father and uncle after dragging them from the palace. David's ears rang again with the shouts and jeers of the crowd that echoed off the buildings that day. As he crossed the square, he did not permit himself to look at the Tolbooth for fear that his rage would spill over and give him away.

He turned into one of the narrow, sloping passageways that cut through the tall buildings on either side of the High Street and found a dark doorway with a direct view of the Tolbooth. Only then did he lift his gaze.

Though he had known what to expect, his stomach churned violently at the sight of the two grisly heads on their pikes. His body shook with a poisonous mix of rage and grief as he stared at what was left of his father. They had made a mockery of the man David had admired all his life. His father's sternly handsome features were distorted in a grimace that looked like a gruesome grin, his dark gold hair was matted, and flies ate at his bulging eyes.

David's chest constricted until his breath came in wheezes. He wanted to fight his way into the palace, wielding his sword and ax until he killed every man in sight. But Regent Albany, the man who ordered the execution, was no longer in the palace, or even in Scotland.

In any case, David had too many responsibilities to give in to thoughtless acts that would surely result in his death. He was the new Laird of Wedderburn, and the protection of the entire Hume clan fell to him. When he thought of his younger brothers and how much they needed him, he finally loosened his grip on his dirk, which he'd been holding so tightly that his hand was stiff.

The execution of the two Hume lairds and this humiliating display of their heads made their clan appear weak and vulnerable. That perception put their clan in even greater danger, and so David must change it. This first step toward that end required stealth, not his sword.

He would have his bloody vengeance, but not today.

While he waited for nightfall, he pondered how Regent Albany had managed to prevail over men who were better than him in every way that should matter. The first time Albany captured David's father and uncle, they persuaded their jailor, a Hamilton, to free them and join the queen's side. A furious Albany responded by having their wives taken hostage.

108

David wondered if Albany understood at the time just how clever that move was, or if he had merely taken the women out of spite. In any event, the trap was set.

By then, Albany was planning to return to France, which was more home to him than Scotland. David's uncle was inclined to wait and seek the women's release from Albany's replacement. But David's father and stepmother had a rare love, and he was tortured by the thought of her suffering in captivity. Because of his weakness for her, he persuaded his brother to accept the regent's invitation and guarantee of their safety.

"Free my wife! Avenge us!" his father had shouted to David as the guards dragged him away.

His father's final words were burned into his soul. While he kept his vigil in the doorway, they spun through his head again and again. He wanted to smash his fist into the wall at the thought of his stepmother living amongst strangers when she learned of her husband's death. Nothing could save the man who held her hostage now. Vengeance was both a debt of honor David owed his father and necessary to restore respect for his clan.

When darkness finally fell on the city, David gave coins to the prostitutes who had gathered nearby and asked them to cause a disturbance. They proved better at keeping their word than the regent. While the women created an impressive commotion, screaming that they had been robbed, David scaled the wall of the Tolbooth.

Gritting his teeth, he jerked his father's head off the pike and placed it gently in the cloth bag slung over his shoulder. He swallowed against the bile that rose in his throat and forced himself to move quickly. As soon as he had collected his uncle's head, he dropped to the ground and left the square at a fast pace. He could still hear the prostitutes shouting when he was halfway to the gate.

A short time later, he reached the tavern outside the city walls where his men waited for him. His half-brothers must have been watching the door, for they ran to greet him as soon as he opened it. Will threw his arms around David's waist, while Robbie, who was four years older, stood by looking embarrassed but relieved. David should admonish Will for his display in front of the men, but he did not have the heart. The lad, who was only ten, had lost his father and missed his mother a great deal.

"I told ye I'd return safe," David said. "I'll not let any harm come to ye, and I will bring your mother home."

Their mother was being held at Dunbar, an impregnable castle protected by a royal garrison. While David did not yet know when or how he would obtain her release, he would do it.

He planned his next moves on the long ride back to Hume territory. In the violent and volatile Border region, you were either feared or preyed upon. David intended to make damned sure he was so feared that no one would ever dare harm his family again.

He would take control of the Hume lands and castles, which had been laid waste and forfeited to the Crown. And then he would take his vengeance on the Blackadders, the scheming liars. While pretending to be allies, the Blackadders had secretly assisted in his stepmother's capture and then urged Albany to execute his father and uncle. It was a damned shame that the Laird of Blackadder Castle was beyond David's reach in a new grave, but his rich lands and widow were ripe for the taking.

And the widow was a Douglas, sister to the Earl of Angus himself. For a man intent on establishing a fearsome reputation, that made her an even greater prize.

ABOUT THE AUTHOR

Margaret Mallory is the award-winning author of the two Scottish historical series, THE DOUGLAS LEGACY and THE RETURN OF THE HIGHLANDERS, and the medieval trilogy, ALL THE KING'S MEN. Her historical romances have won numerous honors, including a RITA© nomination, RT Book Reviews' Best Scotland-Set Historical Romance Award, the National Readers' Choice Award, and two Maggies.

Margaret abandoned her career as a lawyer to become a romance novelist after she realized she'd rather have thrilling adventures with handsome Highland warriors than write briefs and memos. Margaret lives with her husband in the beautiful Pacific Northwest, which looks a lot like parts of the Scottish Highlands. Now that her children are off on their own adventures, she spends most of her time writing, but she also loves to read, watch movies, hike, and travel.

Readers can find information on all of Margaret's books, photos of Scotland, historical tidbits, and links to Margaret on Facebook and Twitter on her website, www.MargaretMallory.com.

Made in the USA
Lexington, KY
12 March 2018